The Red Veil Diaries

Bewitch Me

Marianne Morea

Coventry Press Ltd.

Coventry Press Ltd.
Somers, New York
http://www.coventrypressltd.com

ISBN13: 978-1-7325262-2-8
First Edition: Coventry Press Ltd. 2019

Printed in the USA

"For women, the best aphrodisiacs are words. The G-spot is in the ears. He who looks for it below there is wasting his time."
—*Isabel Allende, Of Love and Shadows*

Chapter One

"*T*his place is off the chain, Laney! Holy beefcakes! Just look at all that man candy! Every size and flavor." Eve Kent licked her lips, practically bouncing in her seat in the VIP lounge. "Some friend, keeping this to yourself."

Lane Alden matched Eve's grin. "It's an underground vampire club for a reason, Evie. We know what's what, but the rest of the world?" She shook her head. "Not so much, and the undead want to keep it that way. A secret in plain sight. Technically, *we're* not even supposed to be here."

On the surface, the Red Veil was a trendy hangout for A-listers and wannabes who liked to think they lived on the edge. A mix of raw fantasy and kickass music wrapped in a big Goth bow. In truth it was also the seat of New York's Vampire Council, but that knowledge was on a need to know basis. A tidbit most hadn't a clue.

"I never realized vampires were so…so…" Eve trailed off, craning her neck for a better view of the main floor.

"Tempting?" Lane replied with a laugh. "Close your mouth, Eve, you're drooling."

With a sheepish chuckle, she wiped the corner of her mouth with the back of her hand. "Can you blame me? Talk about looking like you walked off the pages of a magazine." She took a quick breath. "I mean, I know the club is crawling with celebrity impersonators just for fun, but Holy Cinemascope! James Dean and Marlon Brando! Where did they find them?"

Lane wrapped her hand around her frosted mug and followed Eve's line of sight. "They're pretty amazing, but they're not impersonators."

Eve pulled her eyes from the crowd, her mouth dropping. "Wait, are you saying—"

"Yup."

Skeptical, Eve slid her gaze to the 50s icons again, before zeroing in on another celeb. "So, you're telling me, Patrick Swayze over there—" She gave a slow chin pop toward the end of the bar. "Mr. *Dirty Dancing* himself. *He's* the real deal? Big as life and thirty feet away from where we sit?"

"Depends on how you define *life*, but otherwise—" Lane nodded. "They are the original stars, with one major exception. They now drink blood to survive."

Eve blinked, stunned.

Lane lifted her drink toward her lips. "A bit of a shocker, I know. Back in the day, the Vampire Supreme was a huge movie buff. Intervention was a purely selfish move on his part, but when his

favorite stars got sick or had a fatal accident, he made them an offer they couldn't refuse."

"Refuse? When you've got an indiscernible pulse, and you're lying on a slab with a tag on your toe, it's not a time to be choosy." Eve snorted.

Lane sipped her drink. "Sure, it is. But vampires don't worry about annoying credos the way we do."

"An it harm none, do as ye will." Eve's reply was a rote whisper.

"Exactly. Plus, the concept of personal gain isn't a problem for the undead, either. Still, it's kind of cool knowing our pop icons aren't really gone. Speaking of which, I ran into Alan Rickman a couple of months ago."

Eve exhaled a wistful sigh. "After all this time? *Always.*"

"I love that."

"Me, too." Eve nodded, finishing what was left of her martini. "Still, an undead Professor Snape is something I could believe." She paused holding the stem of her glass. "Laney, you said the 'Vampire Supreme.' Did you mean Sebastién DuLac? The one who just died?"

Lane bobbed her head. "Sebastién was a giant, condescending prick, but he was also a closet red-carpet groupie." She shrugged again. "Rubbing elbows with the elite fed his ego. Human or supernatural, he collected them. Especially if they

had an ability he envied or found fascinating. He befriended Sean Leighton, Alpha of the Brethren of Were, just to get to his mate. Lily is a psychic, but Sebastién was convinced she could walk between worlds."

"Like between the living and the dead, or between our plane and Faerie?"

"Between the living and the dead," Lane replied, "but I wouldn't be surprised if he thought Lily could waltz into the Fae realm unhindered."

"Did Sebastién get her, or did the alpha rip him to shreds?"

Lane smirked at the gossipy look on Eve's face. "Sean Leighton is a powerful alpha, and the hottest shifter I've met, but Lily can hold her own. Sebastién couldn't lay a finger on her."

Eve slid her gaze back toward the bar. "Do you think he might—" Eve shook her head, not finishing her thought.

"Who might *what*?" Lane asked with a smirk.

She shook her head again. "Forget it. He's *Dirty Dancing*'s Johnny Castle, and I'm a chubby witch with mousy brown hair and ordinary brown eyes."

"Evie, stop that."

"Laney, I've spent so much time cooped up in the motherhouse library, my ass now has its own zip code. If it wasn't for the rush of blood through my veins, my pasty skin could pass for undead. Hell, I'm surprised I don't hiss at daylight." She

offered a soft shrug. "I'm not like you. You're fair and willowy. Members of the Circle of the Raven may be Fae-kissed, but I must have been absent when they handed out the *look*." Eve crooked her fingers into quotes.

"You don't give yourself enough credit, Evie. Forget dirty dancing with the vampires. Half the time the trace amount of Fae blood in our veins is too much of a distraction. They can't help themselves. Shifters on the other hand are a different story.

"You're a pretty girl, with just the right curves to drive the fanged and furry set wild. Focus on them. They love a little meat on the bone. As for your hair, it's a rich chestnut, and your eyes are more amber than brown." Laney reached for her friend's hand. "I mean it, Evie. No more self-deprecating. You're a Blood Witch about to join the Circle of the Raven, and we're a picky bunch of witchy bitches. Roll with that."

Eve sniffed, giving Laney a weedy smile. "At least I don't have pencils stuck in a messy bun or my nose in a book."

"Exactly. Now let go and relax. We're here to have fun. I'd say be careful, but you and I have nothing to worry about. At least not with the undead set. Vampires might have a hard time resisting our blood, but unless they want to chance the inherent risk, I think we're safe."

"What do you mean?"

Lane considered her friend. "Truth is, witch blood is poisonous to some vampires. It's a double whammy with Fae-kissed witches, because our blood is inherently alluring. Almost a drug. A plus for being a Raven if push came to shove in a dark alley."

"How come this isn't in any book I've studied? Believe me, I've combed through plenty."

"There isn't a spell for everything, Eve. We learn through trial and error. Witches need to adapt quickly. To cast on the fly and conjure when needed. Your initiation into the Circle of the Raven and our motherhouse is only the beginning.

"Anyway, I'm glad the Red Veil meets with your approval. Just remember, when it comes to the icy hot vampires, you look but don't touch. Like I said, Weres and shifters are a different story." Lane winked, turning an eye toward a sexy, wide-shouldered Were at the other end of the bar. "Touch all you want, as often as you want."

The crowd was thick and animated as they overlooked the main floor. A server approached with a smile and a small round tray.

"Can I get you ladies another drink?"

Lane nodded, draining the last of her mug. "I'll have another Moscow Mule. Extra ginger and lime this time."

"That one's my favorite," she said, before turning to Eve. "And you?"

"I'll try a dirty martini this time." She rubbed her hands together. "Three olives and heavy on the dirty."

The server grinned. "Got it. Coming right up, but I'll have to see some I.D. first."

"I showed the other server when we first ordered."

The server shrugged. "House rules. Sorry."

Eve grumbled, fishing in her purse. "I can't wait until they don't ask anymore."

"Yes, you can." Laney shook her head with a chuckle. "Trust me, it's as bad as the first day you get called ma'am."

The server looked at Eve's driver's license and then handed it back with another nod. "Thanks. I'll be right back with your drinks."

"Why couldn't you put the whammy on her the way you did the VIP bouncer?"

Lane glanced over her shoulder at the tall Were manning the velvet rope. "Because, proving you're over twenty-one is simple. Getting into the VIP section of the Red Veil, not so much." She smoothed the fresh napkin in front of her. "Magic is all about balance, Evie, and just because you *can*, doesn't always mean you should. The warning for witches about magic for personal gain is true, to a certain extent."

"So, getting the bouncer to let us into the VIP section isn't personal gain?"

Lane grinned. "Okay, so I bent the rules a little with that, big deal. I've been here a lot this past year. Is it *my* fault the bouncer recognized me? Technically, *he* allowed the perk."

"Yeah, right. With a little help from a handy compulsion spell. Was that what you meant about casting on the fly?"

"Wiseass." Lane smirked at the young witch.

The server came back with their drinks, setting them on the table. "This round is on the house." She turned with a grin toward the bouncer at the bottom of the stairs. "You must have made quite an impression on Kyle. He's usually so tight with money, he squeaks."

Eve stifled a snicker and Lane shot her a look. "Tell him we said thank you, and we'll catch up with him later."

The server walked away, and Lane turned to make eye contact with the bouncer.

"Watch and learn, little girl." Lane circled her hand in a small clockwise orbit, muttering in Latin under her breath. She maintained eye contact with Kyle, and in seconds he blinked as though confused, and then looked away.

"And that's how it's done. No harm, no foul." Lane picked up her drink, clicking her tongue. "Sometimes it's good to be a witch."

No sooner had the words left her mouth, than heat scorched her lungs. Her hand flew to her chest and she sucked in a painful breath.

"You okay?" Eve asked, lowering her drink.

Vertigo gripped hard and fast and she dropped her drink, fumbling for the edge of the table, taking short, sharp breaths.

"Lane!" Eve pushed back in her chair. "Help! Someone!"

The server rushed over, and they both moved to either side of Lane's chair. "What's the matter?" she asked.

"I don't know. She was fine a moment ago."

The server spared a look for the bartender watching from the sidelines. "Maybe we should call an ambulance. Is she allergic to anything? Asthmatic? Did she take…something?"

"She's not a druggie," Eve shot back, wrapping a hand around Lane's shoulder. "She's a witch, like you're a shifter, so help me get her out of this crowd so we can figure out what's happening."

The server straightened, surprised. "A witch? You're not supposed to—"

"Not supposed to what?" She glared up at the woman. "Are you going to help, or just stand pointless and watch?"

The woman scrambled, taking Lane's other arm. "Of course. Sorry," she replied. "The manager's office has a couch. Follow me."

Marianne Morea

Lane squeezed her eyes closed, ignoring the squabbling women. Something or someone in the club was messing with her senses. But why?

Clearing her mind, she focused on her breathing. In, out. In, out, until the vertigo ebbed. The music pulse still vibrated on her skin, and the air was thick as it skimmed her body, but she was in control.

"C'mon, Laney. Let's get you some place quiet with less nosy parkers." Eve hooked her arm inside Lane's elbow, but Lane shook her head.

She exhaled and then opened her eyes. "Give me a minute, Eve. I'm okay." Vodka and melting ice dripped off the edge of the table, chilling her fingers, and she let go for a moment only to grab hold again when she tried to stand.

"That's it. You need some fresh air and that means we're outta here. I'm calling an Uber."

Lane dragged in a steadying breath. "It's passing. Truly."

"Do you want me to call someone for you?" the server asked.

The three stood in the middle of a not so oblivious crowd. Lane shook her head again, letting go of the table for good.

"Thanks, but that's not necessary. I'm okay." Lane took another breath. "It's probably a backlash for tipping the VIP scales and then being so glib about it."

The server offered a tight smile, mopping up what was left of the spill. "I'll bring you some fresh drinks."

Plopping the wet bar towel into Lane's empty copper mug, she looked directly at Lane. "If you're sure you're okay."

"Yes, thanks. And a drink is just what the witch doctor ordered." She offered the woman a quick smile.

The server turned for the bar and Lane picked up Eve's martini, gulping a deep sip. "Talk to me, Evie. Tell me how your studies are going. Anything." She winced again, her hand going to her temple. "Any questions you want to ask?"

Eve threw a wet, crumpled napkin at her friend. "Questions? Yeah, I'd say I have a few. Like what the hell happened? One minute you're pulling a mind freak on the bouncer, and the next you're holding on for dear life. I may be a coven initiate, but I'm not stupid. That was no mere backlash. I mean, you're older and more skilled, but I can handle it. Tell me."

"Drink your martini, Eve." She handed the younger witch her glass. "It *was* a backlash. I played fast and loose with our Wiccan rules and ignored the whole personal gain tenet. Karma is a toothy bitch, and this time she answered in real time."

"You think?" Eve smirked at her friend.

Lane flashed a sheepish grin, but her gut still churned. If that was a consequence for nerve, then why did it feel so slick?

"I know you, Lane Alden, but I have no choice but to trust you. Just promise you'll fess up if we head into real trouble or something."

"Deal."

She smiled at her friend, but uncertainty bit at her belly. If that oily spin was a karmic bitch-slap, then so be it. But if it wasn't?

Chapter Two

*T*he server returned with two fresh drinks and put them on the table. Lane gave the woman a quick smile and then picked up her drink, eyeing the younger Raven. Eve had gone quiet, but her eyes said otherwise.

"You look like you 've got a question burning. You can ask me anything, Eve. Really."

"It's stupid. Just forget it."

Lane sighed. "C'mon, Eve. You watched me take a karmic thump in public, and I'm the elder at this table."

Eve gave her a droll look. "Twenty-eight doesn't qualify you for Crone, Laney."

"Very funny. Now spill."

Pulling her martini glass closer, she hesitated, smoothing the napkin under its stem. "Okay, but I told you it was stupid."

"I'm waiting."

"Do you think regular people sensed what was up with you? I mean, do they even know?"

"Know what?"

Eve inched closer, lowering her voice. "That this place is for real. As in *Original Gangstas*. Fangs and all."

Eve bared her teeth with a Bela Lugosi style hiss, and Lane lost it, sputtering on her drink. She grabbed her napkin to clean her chin, laughing.

"I told you it was stupid." Eve made a face.

Lane wiped her mouth and the front of her sleeve. "Oh, man. That was too funny. Still, I doubt vampires have ever been referred to as *Original Gangstas*, especially not when the Fae have owned the title since before time began."

"Witch 101. I get it. Dumb question." Eve fidgeted with her napkin.

"Every one of us has wondered the same thing from time to time. As clever as humans can be, they are still mired in a millennium of superstition and religious prejudice. They fear what they don't understand and hate what they fear. Even amongst themselves.

"So, as for your not-so-dumb question, if I had to venture a guess, it would be a hard no. I doubt regular people grasp the paranormal realities staring them in the face. Humans like to play with the idea of the supernatural, but most would freak if they knew what bellied up to the bar gauging their blood type."

Eve turned her gaze toward the dance floor. "Maybe they'd love knowing the supernatural

exists outside the movies. I mean, talk about a fantasy come true, and—" Her mouth dropped, clipping the rest of her words. "Oh, my goddess. I think my ovaries just exploded."

Lane chuckled, licking lime juice from her thumb. "Looks like the idea of fantasies coming true isn't just for humans."

"Jeez. Is he for *real*?"

Lane tracked Eve's line of sight, watching a hunkie Were walk to the bar and order. "Oh, honey. That is *very* real."

"Be still my throbbing vagina."

Lane stifled a laugh. "Throbbing? Good word."

"Shut up, Lane. You should talk."

"No, I'm serious. The Red Veil is a place for guilty pleasures. The important thing is to be in the moment, right here, right now. Partake of all kinds, human and supernatural alike."

Eve licked her lips. "I'd like to partake of him, right here, right now."

Lane hid her smirk behind her mug's copper rim. She couldn't blame the girl's open-mouthed stare. There were panty-dropping hotties everywhere you looked. Perhaps the Veil's vampire owners planned it that way. A new strategy to lure in fresh blood. More bang for the fang.

"People should take a walk on the wild side from time to time. You should go for it, Eve."

The young witch jerked her eyes back to Lane. "And that's code for what, exactly?"

"To paraphrase Lady Gaga, when it comes to love, if it's not rough it isn't fun." She shrugged. "Keeps things interesting."

"I bet. From what I've seen so far, I'm sure it's not hard to find a playmate."

Lane winked. "Easier still, if you have a certain magical skill set. Still, this isn't just about finding a fuckboy for hot monkey sex. Some of the best underground bands play here before they hit it big. Plus, the Veil makes the best Moscow Mule in the city."

"Yeah, nice try."

"Seriously, Eve. Vampire lust aside, the club part of this place is straight up legit. Real bands, real booze, and real bouncers who love to get busy on anyone trying to color outside the lines. The undead allow plenty of tease, but no follow through when it comes to blood sport. At least not out in the open."

"Now *that* sounds interesting." Eve scooted in, all ears.

Lane shook her head.

"Oh, c'mon. I know you know."

Lane shrugged, finishing her drink. "I do know, but that information is strictly on a need to know basis, and right now you *don't* need to know." She

paused, letting a slow grin curve. "At least not until *after* you pass your initiation, little Raven."

"Party pooper."

They relaxed into the night, finally comfortable enough to enjoy the music and foreplay-in-motion out on the dance floor.

Lights flashed and the band went into a cover of The Cure's "Love Song." Eve bopped in her chair to the beat, singing low and off key with the rest of the crowd.

The simple lyrics spoke quiet volumes. Home again. Whole again. Lane closed her eyes. Those were anchors that eluded her, despite her magic. She never quite fit. Anywhere. At least not fully.

Not since—

She shook her head, dismissing the regret threatening to kill her buzz. Not here. Not now.

The Red Veil was her perfect escape. A blend of macabre and ethereal beauty wrapped in a veil of raw need. Its notorious backrooms were another story, though. They were by invitation only, and the only place on premises where people went to lose themselves between blurred erotic lines.

She'd been lucky to participate a few times, but there was no chance in hell they'd let a Fae-kissed witch and a coven initiate through those well-guarded doors tonight. No matter how eager.

Still, backlash or not, backrooms or not, Eve seemed to enjoy herself, and that was the point.

Lane lifted her empty mug in salute. "To the first of your many milestones, Eve—and to the Red Veil. Our little secret."

"Secret?" Eve pulled her martini back from the toast. "Why?"

"Because it will cause a headache for me, and I don't want to deal with a headache," she explained without explaining

No wonder Caitlan said this crop of initiates was more difficult than the ones any other year. Too many questions.

"That makes no sense. Our coven is top heavy with females, Laney. And I don't mean in a big titty city kind of way. The Circle of the Raven is New York's motherhouse. As in the divine feminine. Read the subtext. It screams not enough men, in big capital letters."

"Don't make me regret bringing you tonight, Eve. You've got to swear not to say a word to anyone. I'm serious. If Caitlan finds out I brought you here, forget guys hot enough to burn, she'll break protocol and burn *me* at the stake. I'm already in her book as a bad influence. She'll light the pyre with one angry look, and then dance on my ashes if she finds out."

Eve laughed. "Dramatic much? Caitlan's not the kiss my ring type, so there must be a good reason you think she'd draw such a hard line. Maybe

something to do with a bad influence's guilty pleasures?"

"Good witch or bad, it doesn't make what I said any less true. The undead that run this joint haven't exactly welcomed our kind, but truces are forming between unlikely supernaturals all over the place. Just look at the tentative peace between the Weres and the vampires. So, I figured why not?

"That truce was born out of literal necessity, Lane. HepZ was horrible. We're lucky the outbreak didn't reach the witchy community. It would have wiped us out in weeks. Being afraid of Caitlan and her rules or the club and its consequences are not the same thing."

So much for relaxing in VIP comfort. The club and its consequences? The witchling really hadn't a clue.

"You said you've been cooped up studying for weeks." Lane tried a different tack. "Blood Witch Lore is no joke. Back in the day, the only thing that kept my nose in the books was the guarantee of free-range magic once I passed."

"I know, but—"

The Circle of the Raven was the most powerful coven in New York, and the reason their supreme was no joke. Eve's obstinance was fallout from the stress of her initiation, but she'd rather deal with a rebellious Raven than their angry supreme any day.

Caitlan, on the other hand, was slightly to the left of the Wicked Witch of the West when it came to initiates hitting the books. But all work and no play made for a sad practitioner. Eve needed a diversion. A two-legged and hung like a horse kind of diversion. Even if it meant taking Caitlan's dagger-eyed stare.

Eve went quiet again, watching the purple light cast shadows along the poured concrete dance floor. Ambient light set the club's red boudoir feel to almost black. A perfect contrast to the bar's shiny steel and chrome.

"What does it feel like?" she asked, finally.

"What does what feel like?"

"To have all that power at your fingertips?"

Lane dug for the lime at the bottom of her mug, plopping it in her mouth. She chewed on the tart fruit before putting the rind on her napkin.

"You have power now, Eve. It's part of your DNA. An initiation simply assures the coven you're ready to wield it properly. Controlling your power instead of *it* controlling *you*. You'll find out what I mean soon enough. In the meantime, why not put some of what you studied into practice?"

"But—"

"Pfft." Lane dismissed the halfhearted argument. "You need a break, Eve. Why else do you think I risked my ass bringing you here, if not to try out some of your tricks?" She shrugged.

"Who's going to know? And since I can't stop you from blabbing, at least there'll be something to show for my trouble."

"Wow, you make me sound like a brat."

"Well, if the broom fits, ride it."

"Hey!"

Lane chuckled. "Seriously. Do something for yourself tonight. I would, if I were you. In fact, I have. Many, many times. That shifter at the bar is yours for the taking. Hell, if I can smell the pheromones pouring off you, you know he certainly does.

"Well, Miss Ovaries Exploded? Do your stuff. Make eye contact and hold. Imagine the taste of his mouth. The way his fingers feel on your skin. Trust me, Eve. If you're in control, tonight might be a night you never forget."

Eve spared a glance for the handsome Were. "You think? I've never done anything like this before. I mean, he's definitely worth straddling six ways to Sunday, but—"

"No buts. We're not playing by the rules tonight. Focus your gaze and will him to turn. Once he does, he's yours. Go for it."

Taking a breath, Eve nodded. She stared at the man's back until his hand rose to the nape of his neck. When he turned, she locked eyes with his and mumbled a soft spell. In seconds, he picked up his drink and headed toward them.

"Holy shit! It actually worked." She swallowed hard. "What do I do now?"

"Don't break eye contact. When he stops at the table, *you* speak first. Tell him what you want and then visualize it happening. He'll get the picture in vivid detail once you put it in his mind."

The shifter stopped at Eve's chair with a confused look on his face. He stood holding his drink but didn't say anything.

Eve kept eye contact, but Lane had to smack her on the arm to get her to breathe. "*Uhm,* that looks interesting. What are you drinking?"

He blinked, but then glanced at the long neck in his hand. "It's called a Purple Haze. The brewery is in Louisiana."

Lane had to look away. Spelled or not, the boy didn't seem the sharpest knife in the drawer.

"I bet," Eve added. "The Mardi Gras funeral skeleton on the label is really cool."

He licked his lips but didn't say anything else.

"Are you visiting New York?" She bit her lip against a nervous giggle. "I'm Eve, by the way." She held out her hand, stifling a quick gasp when he folded her fingers into his palm.

"No, I'm from Long Island City. I'm Mason—" He paused, shaking his head. "You know, I'm not exactly sure how I ended up talking to you. One minute I'm sipping my beer at the bar, and the next nothing mattered except meeting you." He

hesitated again, but this time with a smile. "Not that I'm sorry."

"Me neither," she replied. "You know—" She leaned in, giving him an eyeful of cleavage. "I love this place. The music rocks, and I really love to dance. You?"

A slow, grin tugged at the shifter's mouth. "I know exactly what you mean."

"So, do you like to dance?"

Eve murmured something more, and Mason's semi-perplexed look changed to a hungry stare. She nearly choked.

"There's nothing I'd like more." He chuckled then, rubbing a finger under his full bottom lip. "Actually, that's not true. If I told you what ran through my mind when I walked over, you'd slap me."

"That bad, huh?"

"No, that good. As in *X-rated* good." Mason hesitated again. "Look, I'm not always this forward. Not unless it's a full moon." He exhaled, still unsure. "I can't explain it, but I can't fight it, either." His gaze flicked from her face to her deep décolleté. "Not that I'd want to...God, you look good enough to eat."

She laughed. "Don't tell me. Wolf, right?"

"*Howl* you doing?" he replied, cracking a grin. "So, you're one of us, then. At least, I hope so. It'll save time explaining the unexplainable."

"We are—" Lane quietened a laugh. "Same tree, different branch, though."

"Mason, this is my friend—"

"Lane," she interjected. "Who was just about to head to the bar."

"Laney, no—"

With a dismissive wave, Lane pushed herself from her chair. "I'll be back. Just don't do anything I wouldn't do."

"Ha. That leaves things wide open, Miss I like to play rough sometimes."

Mason raised an eyebrow, glancing between the two witches. "Wow. And I thought tonight was going to be a bust. Lucky me. Two for the price of one."

He took a step back, giving Eve another suggestive look before sliding some of that steam to where Lane stood.

"Hold up, cowboy." Lane raised an eyebrow, shutting him down.

Eve's projection clearly overshot the mark. Either that or the horndog was truly as thick as a brick. Three was definitely *not* company, no matter what wolf boy thought.

"You've got the wrong end of the stick here, pup. So, unless you want to end up with a permanent tail, I suggest you keep your eye on one prize." She glanced at Eve. "Or do I need to conjure a rolled-up magazine and whack you on the nose?"

Mason burst out laughing.

"I think this was my bad." Eve winced, mouthing sorry to Lane.

"No worries, babe. I still make out the winner tonight." He lifted Eve's hand to his lips, skimming her knuckles. "Besides, I'm dying to see if the images in my head match what I see in your eyes."

Lane's phone buzzed and she dug in her back pocket, saved by the cell. "Shit. It's Caitlan." She made a face at the name on caller I.D. Their supreme had precognition, but damn she was good.

"What should I do?" Eve asked.

Lane waved the two of them down. "I have to take this or Caitlan will materialize or worse. Drinks are on me. Just don't go anywhere until I get back." Turning on her heel, she pressed accept call.

"Caitlan?" She kept her tone light, plugging her opposite ear as she walked from the table. "What's up?"

"Where are you?"

"I'm out, why?"

"Out where?"

Lane peered around a chrome pillar only to see Eve walking with Mason down the VIP stairs toward the dance floor.

"Shit," she muttered.

"Funny how one word can give so much away. What are you up to, missy?"

Lane frowned, turning her attention to the call. "Caitlan, did you call just to annoy me? I told you I'm out. I'm not one of your initiates, so go hound them."

"I would, but they're nowhere to be found. If this is one of your stunts, Lane Alden—"

"What makes you think missing initiates have anything to do with me?" She exhaled. "You know what, don't answer that. While I appreciate the backhanded vote of confidence that I could organize a Coven *coup de grâce*, I don't know what you're talking about, Caitlan. Your girls are doubtless holed up somewhere with a pizza and a cheap bottle of wine. That's what my friends and I did before our initiation."

"Exactly my point."

Lane scooted around the edge of the bar, trying to keep Eve in sight. "Caitlan, stop worrying. Your witchlings are all of age. If they needed to blow off a little steam, so what? Their test is at the end of the week. Every one of them will show up bright-eyed and bushy-tailed for their Dawning Ceremony. Have you ever known a Raven to miss their moment?"

"No, but—"

"Exactly," Lane shot back, watching Mason and Eve give each other a tongue bath on the dance floor. "Look, I have to go."

"Wait, Lane—*please*."

That got her attention. She didn't hang up, but she wasn't sure she wanted to know what prompted their usually hard-assed supreme to be so imploring.

"You there?" Caitlan prompted.

Lane chewed on her lip. "I'm here. What's going on, Caitlan?"

"I need to talk with you." The supreme hesitated. "About a blood rite."

"A blood rite? You can't be serious. Why?"

"Word reached me about an hour ago. It's why I'm so frantic. There's an Unseelie in the city."

"Caitlan, there are any number of Sidhe, Seelie and Unseelie, in the city at any given time. Why is this a cause for alarm?"

"This one is a rogue, and he's looking to claim anyone with Fae-kissed blood."

"Claim? How? Why?" Lane sank into the nearest chair. "What did you hear?"

"There was an incident in the Dark Court. Some sort of power struggle or failed coup against the Unseelie king. I don't know all the details, but the Sidhe responsible was banished, accused of scandal. The price for him to regain his place at court is to seize a Fae-kissed witch and return with them to Faerie."

Caitlan's words came in a frustrated rush. Lane raked a hand through her long blonde hair. "For what purpose? I've never heard such a thing."

"Your guess is as good as mine." Caitlan exhaled on the other end of the phone. "Anyway, the why of it doesn't matter. We must do something. Dark Sidhe aren't known for kindness."

"Against humans. Not against their own."

Caitlan grunted, and the sound was both resentful and weary. "Despite the trace in our blood, we're not Fae. No court has ever claimed our lineage. In their eyes, Fae-kissed witches are a humiliation, only slightly better than humans. Maybe that's part of the so-called scandal."

The supreme was quiet for a moment before continuing. "I have no other choice, Lane. I am recalling all coven members to the motherhouse. Speculation is of no use, and we're wasting time. We need to protect our own, and the best way to do that is a lockdown and a blood rite. So, if you know the whereabouts of any of our initiates—" The leader of the Circle of the Raven didn't need to finish.

"I understand."

"Good." Caitlan paused again. "And Laney—"

"Yes?"

"Be careful, honey."

The supreme's voice softened, and for a moment it held the same gentleness Lane remembered from when she came to the motherhouse as a child. She had no memory of what came before, but all Fae-kissed witches were

destined for the Circle of the Raven, and despite the supreme's penchant for discipline, Caitlan did everything she could to make their transition seamless and natural for every witchling.

Still, Lane was no longer a child, and over the years had given Caitlan and the other elders a run for their money. A black sheep.

"Lane, are you listening?"

She coughed. "Yeah...sorry. I was just thinking."

"Good. Despite you're reckless nature, you're a clever cookie. I know you don't usually like to play by the rules, but in this instance, you need to remember everything I taught you about the Sidhe to keep yourself, and whoever is with you, safe—at least until you're securely behind motherhouse doors. A rogue like this will do anything to regain their position at court. Shapeshift. Even kill." Her voice cracked. "I don't want to lose you. Any of you."

Lane chewed her lip. Caitlan knew Eve was with her tonight. The fact she didn't stop them from sneaking out spoke volumes. Their supreme wasn't quite the hard-ass she wanted everyone to believe. Black sheep or not, Caitlan loved her. And Eve.

"And Laney, if you don't make it home in time, promise you'll find some other kind of—sanctuary."

The word left no question Caitlan knew where she and Eve were tonight, but she also knew vampire council doors were iron clad. Talk about a clever cookie. If they had to face a rogue Sidhe, there was no better place to do so.

Lane closed her eyes, regretting the whole evening. "I'll do what I can, Caitlan. I promise."

Lane pressed end and locked her phone. She turned on her heel to head for the stairs, scanning for Eve the entire way. Caitlan's news explained what skimmed her senses earlier tonight. It wasn't a backlash. It was a premonition. She needed to grab Eve and get out before something happened.

Chapter Three

*T*he last thing Lane wanted was an undead frenzy. Fae blood was intoxicating to vampires, and the possibility of a full-blooded Sidhe in their private playground? Bad. Very bad.

It was enough she spelled their way into the VIP lounge, but to bring trouble to their doorstep was something else.

Vampires were imperious by nature, and not the most forgiving of beings. Especially not with those who disrespected their refuge. The Red Veil wasn't just a trendy underground club. It was *Le Sanctuaire*.

Sanctuary.

A place undead elders, Sebastién DuLac, Rémy Tessier, and Dominic De'Lessep, founded when North America was still the New World. It had evolved over the centuries, but here it stood in its modern incarnation.

Averting an incident in vampire country needed speed and stealth. She needed to work fast and stay as far under the undead radar as possible.

Pushing her way through the throng, Lane craned to peer past the sea of Goth humanity. The last she saw of Eve she was at the center of the pulsing crowd with Mason.

"Hopeless," she muttered, pivoting toward a back corner instead. She wasn't going to find Eve using ordinary means. She needed magic.

The back corridor opposite the bathrooms was quieter, and less likely for her to be interrupted. Leaning against a veil-draped pillar, she closed her eyes and expanded her senses. She concentrated on Eve and their shared bloodline.

Silence. Not even a blip.

Maybe a vampy ward blocked her search. Or maybe Eve's mind was so sex-soaked she didn't want to be found.

Opening her eyes, she exhaled an expletive. "You and your *'go for it'* attitude, Alden. Clever cookie, my ass."

Eve had teased her about their innate scrying ability, calling it a witchy version of Apple's Find My Phone. It was obvious the girl had turned hers to silent.

"I know you're getting your freak on right now, but I need a hint, sweetie. Where are you?" She physically scanned the area once more, hoping for something.

If Mason hurt her, that dumbass shifter would never see another full moon. Lifting a hand to her

forehead, she exhaled. Most Weres were quick-witted as well as attractive. Leave it to her to pick the mental runt of the litter.

"Okay, Evie. I need you to answer me. Now."

For a witch not to answer a summons, it meant one of two things. Either she ignored the call, or she couldn't respond.

Worst case scenarios sprang to life and Lane clenched her jaw. "Stop it. We're not there yet."

Shoving her hand through her hair, she chewed on her lip. She needed to expand her range to the edge of the vampire sanctuary and their infamous backrooms before anything happened.

That's if you're not already too late.

I said stop.

Lane closed her eyes, pushing her guilt to the back of her mind. *We're not playing by the rules tonight.* Well, maybe bending the rules wasn't enough. Maybe she had to break them completely.

Her eyes snapped open.

Screw scrying the periphery. She was getting into those backrooms if it meant force feeding her blood to every vampire trolling the club.

She lifted both hands, her power on full charge, but before she could mumble a spelled word, pins and needles tingled at the base of her spine.

"What the fu—"

Her hands dropped as the tingle spread. It warmed, growing hotter and hotter until it spread through her extremities.

Lane arched away from the pillar. Almost of their own volition, rubbery legs pitched her toward the arched entrance to the backrooms.

Invisible hands trailed the length of her thighs, edging higher and higher. Her breasts ached and wetness slicked the lace of her panties.

Son of a bitch! Someone had answered her summons, but it wasn't Eve.

Her knees went weak, and she fisted the front of her blouse, fumbling for control. The urge to plunge her hands between her legs and self-satisfy nearly drove her to the floor.

The words 'Death by Sex' flashed through her mind, and she forced a breath, steadying herself against the edge of the entry way.

"Fuck you, you bastard!"

A soft chuckle stroked her mind. Except this wasn't funny. It was a taunt. Whoever this was, they wanted her to know they were in control. If it wasn't the rogue Sidhe, it was a minion, and she wasn't about to become a plaything.

What was it she preached to Eve? Witches need to cast on the fly and conjure when required?

Gritting her teeth, she threw a wall up against the invisible mind fuck and marshaled her focus. She reached for the pentacle at her throat and

wrapped her hand around the silver and black tourmaline.

"Hands off, you pig!"

With a snarl, she reversed the attack, sending a bitch slap reply across the highjacked path. A painful hiss echoed in her mind, and she smirked.

"I hope that crushed your balls, you asshole!"

Message clear. Fuck with me and I will fuck with you right back.

She centered her strength before he found a way to retaliate, closing doors all over her mind. She couldn't find Eve without a wide search, but if this fucker kept messing with her mind, her chances were slim to none.

Maybe that was his sick plan. Dark Fae were known to be sexual predators. Death by Sex was a weapon of choice and a badge of honor in the Unseelie Court.

The invasive feel dissipated the moment she shut him down, and she steeled herself, disgusted at the damp feel in her panties.

Her body betrayed her, and she hated that someone had the ability to force her will. Still, score one for Team Witch. The big bad Sidhe bolted the moment she hit back.

"Coward." Drawing a cleansing breath, she used the energy from the crowd as a buffer and braced herself. A solitary witch couldn't go up

against a rogue Sidhe alone. Especially not one with an agenda.

"Yeah, well. Two could play at that game, jerkwad."

She straightened her shoulders. No one touched her without permission, especially not an assailant too chicken to show himself.

The Fae bastard would get more than a bitch-slap when she got hold of him, but right now it was more important she find Eve.

Quieting her mind, she kept herself guarded and her power at low voltage. If opening her senses fully had tipped the bastard to her presence, she'd be damned if she gave him any more help.

"Come out, come out, whoever you are," she murmured. She cast a magical net across the club, pinpointing every supernatural by specific species and position.

Her underlying magic permeated the air, drawing energy from motion and sexual tension. The poured concrete floor shimmered like asphalt in summer, but most patrons moved in the surreal setting completely unaware.

Dread wound its way toward her, floating above the magic. Foreboding black tendrils grew as she followed the ominous sigil toward the entrance to the infamous backrooms.

"Oh God, Eve. No."

She stared at the steel and iron enforced door and her mouth wet dry. "Okay, well. Mason is a shifter. Maybe he has a season pass to a backroom freakshow and everything's all good."

"You really don't believe that, do you?"

Lane whirled on her heel at the deep male timbre. She blinked. The man standing behind her was not what she expected.

"Anyone ever tell you it's rude to eavesdrop on private conversations?"

Tall, gorgeous, and as dark as she was fair, he had supernatural written all over him, despite his cloaked glamour.

"Does it qualify as a conversation when one is talking to themselves?" He cocked his head, flashing a teasing grin.

"Look, I don't have time for whatever it is you think you're doing. I'm not interested. So, go away."

The half-smile on his lips sobered and he met her eyes with a steady, unnerving gaze. "You do realize you'll have to bargain your way through those locked doors. You won't find your charge otherwise. No witch has ever gained access alone. Not without help."

She lifted her chin, sliding into a defensive stance. "If the kind of help you suggest is what I think, there's more than a kick to the balls waiting for you if you take a step closer."

"I'm glad to see time hasn't tempered your devil fire, Laney. Can it be you really don't recognize me?"

Her eyes narrowed. The man's features were strong. With a full mouth and chiseled jaw. His hair was the color of rich dark chocolate, but it was the intense blue of his eyes that held her attention. Eyes the color of Blue Raspberry Crush.

Her chest tightened, and her mouth went dry.

It couldn't be.

He gave a little flourish, finishing with a courtly bow. "Now, love, tell me you don't remember slipping behind the hedgerow with me in Caitlan's garden. Or how we stole a bottle of her best mead and had our own Yule celebration, just us two."

"Gareth?" His name was an uncertain whisper.

Lifting his head, he winked, dropping his glamoured façade. "In the flesh."

Lane blinked again, stunned. "But, you're dead."

"Ah, my love. There's dead, and then there's dead-dead."

Past images flooded her mind as he closed the distance between them. If this was truly Gareth, he was as heady as ever, with the same underlying sensuality that used to make her mouth water.

"But how? I watched you burn." Her words faltered in disbelief, but there he stood. "Are you undead, then?"

It was the only answer that made sense, but there was no hint of vampire in the man. In fact, there was no hint of anything out of the ordinary, except for the fact she watched a pyre consume his body ten years earlier.

"Hardly undead, love." Gareth smiled softly. "You look great, by the way. Ethereal and as gorgeous as ever. You've grown into a stunning woman, Laney. Then again, I'm a little prejudiced. You were mine, so you were perfect. You still are."

"And you still dance around giving straight answers, if it's truly you."

Flashing a crooked smile, he touched the side of his perfect nose. "You were always smarter, but I'll give you a hint. Coveted blood has its advantages."

Her lips parted. "So, it's true then."

"Don't gape, love. It's not your style."

She snapped her mouth shut but slid back into a defensive stance, her eyes narrowing. "Sidhe can shapeshift, and they can help themselves to memories."

"Is this proof enough?" He rolled his shirt sleeve over his forearm, showing her the tender underside.

Lane stared at the mark. The same one she and every other Fae-kissed witch in the Circle of the Raven had upon their initiation. Not a tattoo. Not a brand. An inner mark that rose from their blood.

"Our mark is as unique as it is inborn. Granted by the Goddess Morrigan to the children of a witch and a full-blooded Sidhe and all their descendants. We carry the mark in our blood. Sidhe from either court can conceal almost anything with glamour, but not this."

Lane lifted the belled sleeve of her blouse, holding her forearm out as well. Intricate Celtic spirals twined over soft flesh, climbing ivy-like toward the elbow. Their two marks were identical, and when Lane's arm touched his, the patterns glowed. Like recognized like.

"Do you know how long I wondered and waited?" Her question was barely a murmur. "After a year, I figured the story was just legend. I mourned you, Gareth. For the longest time."

Gareth stroked the soft skin below her mark. "It took me a long time to recover, but yes, the Phoenix did rise."

"Phoenix Fae," she uttered the words almost reverently. "Does Caitlan know?"

He shook his head. "No. No one does." He shrugged. "Well, no one on this plane. Except you."

"This plane." She raised an eyebrow, still skeptical. "Are you saying—"

"Does it matter?" Gareth answered her question with a question. "You want to find your friend, and I want to help. Can't we leave it at that for now?"

She considered him. "Are you going to disappear for another decade, or at least stick around long enough to explain what happened and why you never let me know you were alive?"

Gareth clasped her arm, pressing their marks together. The air shimmered gold around them, soft magic tingling through their bodies.

"No one's making me go anywhere, love." He leaned in closer. "Not this time. Not without you."

The shared tingle spread, enveloping her body in delicious heat. Memories flooded their merged auras, leaving her even more stunned.

Gareth's face tense with need, his hips grinding deep as his thick length filled her. His teasing laugh when he surprised her with their first sex toy.

Her body hummed with pent-up need, and her lips parted again, but not to argue. "Gareth—" Next thing she knew, she was on tiptoe as though ten years never happened, ready to claim his mouth.

He pulled back. "Laney, I—"

She blinked, not sure which stung more. His rejection or her own stupidity. Mortified, she pulled her arm from their combined clasp, but he held tight.

"Laney, don't. Your impulse wasn't wrong. I've missed you. More than you can know. For ten years, you've occupied my mind and my heart." He exhaled, closing his eyes for a moment. "This is my

fault. I shouldn't have tempted you from what's important."

"Tempted me?" Her eyes narrowed, distrust creeping in again. "Gareth, that wasn't you before?"

"Before when?"

With an expletive, her cheeks warmed even more, but she had to ask. "The invisible man touch...thing."

"You've lost me completely."

Self-conscious, she pressed her lips together. "Someone groped me with invisible hands when I tried scrying for Eve. It nearly had me on the floor with my hand in my panties, it was that strong."

Gareth's face tightened. "Fucking Leith."

"Leith." She watched him. "Is he the rogue Sidhe responsible for this mess?"

Nodding, he swore. "Don't worry. I'll show you how to deflect his magic. What he did will never happen again."

"No, it won't." She gave a satisfied snort. "I have a few tricks of my own and reversed it straight back to his balls. Hard."

Gareth laughed, cupping Lane's face. "Still my rebel Raven."

"Yep, only now I have a cause. Let's do what we have to and then blow this blood-pop stand. We have a decade that needs catching up."

Chapter Four

Gareth took Lane by the hand. Power surged between them, enough for her to taste their combined energy on the back of her tongue.

They stood at the entrance to the backrooms, and she held her breath. She'd been in this position before, but always with some Were taking the lead with his tongue down her throat.

"Do you trust me?" Gareth pulled a short-bladed athame from a sheath at his belt, his expression giving nothing away.

She blinked at the glint from the razor-sharp tip. "Wow. I only wanted to kiss you, Gareth. A simple no thanks would have done me fine."

He ignored her attempt at levity and held the athame steady. "Invoke a blood spell, Laney. Then draw the knife edge across my palm." He held the blade out to her hilt first. "You remember how to do that, right?"

"I don't like this, Gareth." She noted the carved handle resting in his palm, with runes and magical sigils she didn't recognize.

He urged the knife closer. "Take the athame, Lane. We're dealing with dark magic, and we need to fight fire with fire. There's only one way we're getting inside this undead citadel, and that's by enticing a vampire to open the door. We don't want to involve another innocent, so it's up to us. If my gut is correct, Eve's date paid a high price for the chance at a piece of witchy ass."

"Do you have to be so crude?" She exhaled a critical breath. Gareth voiced what she already thought. Eve and Mason were in deep shit.

She took the ritual knife from his hand with a less than gracious grunt. "What if this doesn't work?" The hilt buzzed in her palm, latent with power. "Do we have a plan B?"

He didn't answer.

"Blood is never used in white magic, Gareth." She stalled further. "The fates are funny about that. Plus, they never grant exactly what you want. They can be sneaky little beggars, twisting words. Like the Djinn."

"You're right. The fates can be difficult, but in this case, they owe me, Laney. Phoenix blood or not."

She puffed out the last of her indecision. "And you're sure there's no other way? What if we wait for someone to leave and then slip through the door unnoticed? People do it all the time all over the city, and it wouldn't directly involve an innocent."

"Lane, we need to do this on our own. Under our own steam." With a nod, he urged his palm closer to the athame's tip. "Don't be a chicken shit."

"If this goes south—"

"It won't." He nodded again. "Concentrate on what we need to happen, and then cast your best."

There were no more arguments. Lane held her breath and positioned the blade's sharp end over the center of Gareth's palm. Locking eyes with him, she began the summoning spell.

"Hear me in this witching hour, as I intreat the ancient power. Turn the tables, three times three, with banshee's cry reveal the Sidhe. Of Maid, of Mother and of Crone, blood to blood, and bone to bone—"

Gareth's eyes turned a golden hue as she dragged the razor tip across his flesh. A soft line of red formed, and she continued.

"Spirits from the misty veil, I summon forth and avail. From blooded blade safeguard and take, the sacrifice we now make. Magic pure combined and sealed, a captive's path now revealed."

Before he could stop her, Lane twisted the athame around and sliced her own palm as well. Blood pooled, and she clasped her hand to his, mingling their offering.

The ritual steel sandwiched between their palms glowed white hot, sizzling their wounded flesh. Lane hissed at the unexpected pain,

instinctively jerking her hand back, but Gareth tightened his grip, keeping their blood fused.

"Don't let go." His voice left no room for questions.

Lane's throat constricted and she squeezed her eyes closed. Visions played behind her lids with seers' sight.

"Eve!" She winced, trying to sort through fragmented images, swallowing back at the thick smell of blood and sweat in her nose.

The visions ebbed before she could pinpoint anything concrete, but at least now she had a direction.

"Show me where she is, dammit!" With a grunt, Lane jerked Gareth's hand forward with hers, smearing their combined blood on the locked door.

The center steel panel buckled, as vampiric wards crumbled. In seconds, the heavy door swung wide revealing an angry vampire in the entry.

He looked first to Gareth and then to Lane, his nostrils flaring. "The backrooms are off limits to you lot! I don't know how you two managed to offset my wards, but—" The vampire paused midsentence, sniffing his best British highbrow sniff.

Shrewd red eyes flicked from the bloodied door to them and back before he paused, licking his lips. "Is this your best try?" he scoffed, dragging a single finger over the fresh, bloody smear.

Lane opened her mouth to argue, but Gareth pushed her behind his hip, shutting her up.

The vampire licked his finger clean. His red eyes glazed over immediately, and a silly smile replaced his stiff undead upper lip.

The veins in his pallid face glowed a faint blue, and he sighed, putting both hands flat on the door before leaning in to lick it clean.

"Oh, that's lovely. Brilliant." The vampire snorted, half sputter, half giggle, as his posh accent devolved. "Please, sir," he turned glassy eyes to Gareth, "I want some more."

"Listen, Oliver Twist. If you let us through, and then leave us to our business, you may have another taste." Gareth lifted their bloody hands for show and tell. "But only if you don't bother us."

The vampire simpered, resting his cheek on the door's cold surface. "There's much to be bothered with in here." He thumped the door with a limp fist. "Bother, bother, bother."

"Is he drunk?" Lane whispered, stunned.

"That was the plan." He tugged her around to his side, motioning for her to move slowly. "Your spell added power to the Fae trace in our blood, tripling its allure. The effect will wear off soon enough, though vamp-boy will have a doozy of a hangover. I think another little nip will give us the time we need to search for Eve."

Staring at the silly look on the vampire's face, she stifled a laugh when he wiped his nose on his shirt's frilly front brocade. "Oh man. He's drooling like a toothless bulldog."

"Exactly. One drop more and he should pass out completely."

"Gareth, if you're planning what I think, please don't. The undead can't be trusted around fresh blood. Drunk or not, I'm getting a distinct NatGeo Wild vibe. Pulling your wrist back will be like taking a juicy kill away from a starving animal."

"Way ahead of you, love." He winked, slipping a small, clear vial from his pocket. The tiny glass flashed iridescent in the light when he held it up for her to see. "I'm not letting his fangs anywhere near my veins, or yours for that matter."

Letting go of Lane's hand, he held the vial to his wound and folded his fingers into his palm. He squeezed, letting the narrow vial catch the calculated trickle before corking the glass.

"Hey, Dracula, do a witch solid, eh?" Gareth opened his palm and held it outward. "Seal the wound and then leave us be. If you do what we ask, then this is all yours to savor." He held the small glass container between the thumb and forefinger.

The vampire snatched Gareth's palm to his mouth, groaning as he tongued the wound. When finished, he turned red eyes to Lane, but she shook her head.

"No, thanks. I'm good."

Dracula smacked his lips. Defenseless or not, she flinched at his fully descended fangs. She scooted past, letting Gareth finish their transaction.

With all the times she'd been in the backrooms, she'd seen vampires come and go, but never courted one. Telling Eve to look but don't touch wasn't just lip service.

Wincing, she wrapped her injured hand with the black ribbon she wore around neck, using her teeth to pull the knot tight. The burn hurt like hell, but the thin cut had stopped bleeding. Still, she wasn't taking any chances.

"Worked like a charm." Gareth came up beside her wearing a shit-eating grin, gesturing toward the helpless vamp.

She followed his gaze only to see the vampire slumped against the closed reinforced steel like a drunk in an office doorway.

"Maybe we should have left the door open for a quick escape." She smirked. "We can add that to the list for later, along with the other thing."

"What other thing?"

"How you knew the spell and the blood would work." This time, she took him by the hand. "C'mon. I'm taking the lead now."

Despite the crowd in the main club, the backrooms' white marbled anteroom was empty. Telltale sounds from sex play drifted from various

rooms, making her very aware of Gareth's proximity.

He was still the sexiest man she'd ever seen. That she used to know every inch of him intimately wasn't wasted on her, making his closeness even more visceral.

"Interesting place. Reminds me of the ancient brothels in Pompei." He let go of her hand to circle the mosaic floor depicting various sex acts.

She rolled her eyes. "Don't pull the prude card with me, Gareth Fairfax. You forget, I know you pretty well." She stopped herself. Heated memories were making her mouth go dry again. "Or at least I used to."

He slipped his hand into her palm again, careful not to squeeze too hard. "I haven't changed that much. A few scars here and there, but if you play your cards right, I'll let you connect the dots the same way I used to with the freckles on your cheeks."

Her gaze met his, and for a moment it was just the two of them and no one else mattered.

"That's not exactly how I remember that game," she cleared her throat, "but let's not go there right now."

"I wasn't talking about your face, love." He smacked her butt, letting his hand linger.

"If you're going to spank me, Gareth, you better be prepared for whatever comes next. I'm not an

inexperienced girl anymore. I learned a lot in these backrooms."

Gareth stroked her inner elbow. "I've got plenty planned for you, love, and I don't care how many times you've been here. To be honest, it's a turn on." He leaned in, nipping the base of her ear. "Bring on the show and tell."

Lane's body burned with expectation. Her pulse raced and she had to stifle the urge to sink to her knees and lick Gareth's thighs and everything in between.

Clearing her throat again, she removed her arm from his caress and stepped back.

"You want me, Lane."

She met his eyes but didn't reply.

"I feel it in my bones, love. That pull between us. It hasn't changed. From the moment I sensed you, my cock was hard enough to cut diamonds, but your need is even more intense. Is your pretty pink pussy as sweet as I remember?" He nodded. "I plan to find out. When this is over, I'm going to spread you wide, lay you down and pound your soft mound until you scream for release."

"Gareth."

He shook his head, lifting her hand to his lips. "No, Lane. You need to hear this. I want to heal you and hold you and fuck you, because you're mine and I'm yours. The way it should have been before the fates fucked us over."

He kissed her knuckles and then let go of her hand, walking toward one of the tiled archways.

Lane didn't follow.

He glanced back at her hesitation. "If you expect me to apologize for my raw words, forget it. We have a second chance, Lane. I'm not sorry for grabbing it with both hands."

"I'm glad you're not sorry."

He blinked. "Then what?"

"You're going the wrong way."

His mouth opened and closed for a moment. "Why didn't you say something, then?"

"I would have, but you were on a such roll, I didn't want to interrupt." She smirked, stifling a chuckle.

He reached her in two strides, sweeping his arms around her waist. "Bitch."

"Gareth Fairfax, I do believe there's a chink in your perfect armor."

He tightened his grip, letting his lips hover over hers. "You have always been my weakness."

Before she could say a word, he took her mouth, crushing his lips to hers, hard and fast.

Heat zinged through her body and her breath caught in her throat. His kiss was harsh, as though ten years of want had suddenly found release.

She fisted the back of his shirt as his lips plundered her mouth. Lane moaned, meeting his fierce demand with her own. Pushing every

reservation to the back of her mind, she reveled in his taste. It was raw and elemental. Conjuring the spirit of wind and rain, fire, and dark earth, filling her both with primal need and promise.

Gareth's hand dropped from the nape of her neck to caress the curve of her waist. Fingers trailed across thin fabric to seize the weight of her full breast.

"Gareth, stop," she murmured. "Eve—"

He left her vulnerable and wanting, so much so she pulled away. She barely had breath to rein herself in, but she had no choice. If this was where she and Gareth were meant to be, they'd find each other again.

Sliding his hand around her waist, Gareth held her before she slipped past. "Don't pull away, Lane. I didn't come back to hurt you."

"I'm not a fringe benefit, Gareth."

She turned to look away, but he cupped her chin, making her meet his eyes. "And I'm not an opportunist. I haven't changed that much, Laney. Neither have my feelings. You were never on the fringe of anything. Not for me. You were always special. I knew it then, and I know it now."

Lane didn't answer, but she didn't pull away either.

"If you truly don't want me. Don't want this—" He slid his hand to cup her breast again. "Then say the word, and I'll back off."

The choice was hers, and her jaw tightened with uncertainty. Even now, with her panties damp and her nether regions throbbing for his touch, she knew this had to wait.

She chewed on the inside of her cheek. Gareth was still the same gorgeous goofball she knew all those years ago. Of that she was sure. And he was right. She wanted him as much as he wanted her.

"I'm sorry, Lane. You're uncertain, and I should've expected that. Especially under the circumstances." He shook his head, hesitant. "Seeing you again. Knowing in my gut you've wanted me, the way I've wanted you."

Her breath caught at the need in his eyes. "Uhm, maybe we should talk more about this, sooner than later."

"Talk?" He nipped her bottom lip.

"You know what I mean."

His lips curved. "I do. Or at least I hope." He stepped back but kept hold of her hand. "Okay, Witchy Waze. Where are we headed?"

She pointed to the only red-tiled passageway in the antechamber and then took a step toward its entrance.

Gareth held tight, tugging her back.

"What are you doing?" she asked, confused at his hesitation. "This is what I saw in my vision."

He pointed to the inscription above the arch. "I read French, love, and *that* is definitely not welcome to Munchkin Land."

"I know what it means, Gareth. And no, we are categorically *not* in Oz."

The engraved inscription was akin to the warning at the entrance to Hell in *Dante's Inferno.* "Corrupted soul, blood and lust reside within. Enter at your own peril."

She nodded, impressed.

"Obviously, the undead have a penchant for melodrama."

"Not really. This passage is where the undead take the most debauched of their playmates, so it's anything but theatrical. Through here, anything goes. There's even an Oubliette for those that don't make it."

He frowned, staring at the inscription a moment longer. "I wonder if people know what they're getting themselves into. The threshold of no return."

"Plenty of people return, Gareth. They come back for more. Safe words aren't just for BDSM. Consent is key. Same as it is for regular people."

His face was unapologetic. "Regular people don't toss unfortunate partners into an Oubliette, never to be seen again."

She watched his shoulder muscles hunch. "Considering where we are, you might not want to

voice your disapproval too loudly. Especially since the FC is that way." Her gaze tracked the length of the shadowed corridor.

"FC?"

"Fang Central. Otherwise known as the New York Vampire Council, to be precise."

His posture stiffened and darkness shadowed his face for a moment. She watched it war in his eyes and then disappear almost as quickly as it came.

"I didn't mean to give you the wrong impression, and for that I apologize. I've endured blood play for sport, Laney. It's not something I take lightly, regardless of consent."

Guilt slashed, sharp and fast, making her sorry for assuming. Sorry for being so condescending and glib. Ten years was a long time and she had no right to judge.

"I'm sorry, Gareth."

He inhaled a quick breath but managed a soft smile. "I'm in this with you for the duration, but right now my Spidey senses are going nuts, and I you need to stay behind me. I have a few tricks up my sleeve I can't explain, but if things go south, I'll need a clean line of sight."

Lane raised an eyebrow but didn't press. She squeezed his hand, and together they crossed the threshold into the dim unknown.

Chapter Five

"*H*e wants you." Bette stood in the doorway to Abigail's office, her eyes watching the elegant vampire as she studied her computer screen.

"He always wants me." Abigail waggled her eyebrows, still typing. "And I thought vampires were insatiable. Trust me, the fanged and furry got nothing on us—and not just at the full moon." She mimicked a growl.

"Not Dash, Abby. Rémy. He needs to speak to you."

She glanced at her assistant, frowning. "Can't you handle it? If these license renewals don't get paid, the Red Veil will be a G-rated juice bar by Friday night."

"Abby. He's not kidding."

She ignored Bette. "Fucking city bureaucrats. Licenses, my ass. More like extortion, yet we're the bloodsuckers."

"Abigail! Pay attention. A Were died last night. In the backrooms."

Abby's hands stopped mid-keystroke, and she turned, giving her full attention to Bette. "Fuck.

Please tell me it has nothing to do with HepZ. We can't handle another breakout, Bette. Not so soon after everything."

"It's not the virus, Abs. It's worse. I think you'd better let Rémy explain. If you're worried about the club, those licenses are the least of it."

Bette moved to one of the chairs in front of Abby's large desk. "Look, I know you and Rémy prefer to handle things quietly, but this time—"

"This time, what?" Abby looked at her over the top of her laptop.

The younger vampire paused, clearly choosing her words. "This time, I don't think we have a choice to do things our way. There are other parties involved, and our usual means of disposal will," she hesitated, "raise questions we might not want answered."

With an indifferent wave, she went back to her laptop. "Donors know the risk when they sign up for the lifestyle."

"If you say so." Bette fidgeted with the end of her cuff.

Abby looked at her again. "Your fidgeting is screaming a different argument. What aren't you telling me? This incident was accidental, right?"

Bette pressed her lips together.

"Christ's blood on toast!" Abby snatched her phone console closer and buzzed her secretary.

"Yes?" The tinny intercom crackled.

"Calypso, I need you to call—"

Before she could finish her sentence, Bette waved both hands in front of her chest wildly. Abby put the intercom on mute. "What the fuck, Bette?"

"If you're asking her to call Dash, don't. Rémy doesn't want the Weres involved until we know more."

Exhaling hard, Abigail unmuted the intercom. "Never mind, Calypso. I'll take care of this myself."

"No problem, ma'am."

Bette hadn't been undead long enough to let innate vampiric hubris get in the way of common sense. Why else would the council keep her around, if not for the occasional reality check?

Resting an elbow on her desk, Abigail curled a finger over her lip. "Has Rémy seen the body? Be honest. How bad is this?"

The look on Bette's face spoke volumes.

"Lord love a dick." Abigail exhaled, chewing on her lip. She slid open a side desk drawer and pulled out a bottle of Jameson's Black Label and an insulated flask.

"Grab two glasses from the sideboard," she indicated the cherrywood cabinet by the couch. "I think we're both going to need this."

She poured them each a double shot of the aged Scotch before filling the rest with smooth crimson from the flask.

"Bottoms up." Abigail drained her glass in one shot. The warm, fresh blood and whiskey burned through her veins with a comforting feel.

She exhaled, raking a hand through her strawberry blonde hair. "What now?" she said, mostly for her own benefit. "I've never been one to shy away from difficulty, even if it means something unsavory."

"I know."

"We need this like we need our throat ripped out. If the body is as bad as your face says, fear is bound to follow once this gets out."

Bette put her half-finished drink on the desk. "I might as well tell. The body was found in the backrooms. The Carousel Suite in the red zone, to be exact. I had the area secured, but—" She puffed out a quick breath.

"Tell me everything right now. Rémy and I need all the facts if we're going to head off panic in the donor ranks. We haven't had a backroom death in ages."

"Just an observation, Abby. It's nothing."

"Well?"

Bette shrugged. "There was an unusual scent in the air. One I didn't recognize. It rode beneath the scent of residual blood, yet it was so potent it made my nips hard. I couldn't help it. I had to excuse myself and head to my room."

"For what? Did it make you sick?"

Bette shook her head, an embarrassed flush on her pale cheeks.

"For god's sake, Bette. Spit it out."

"Hey, don't shoot the messenger, Ms. Panic Pants. I'm trying to tell you, but this has me freaked out. The scent didn't make me ill. It made me ravenous. For blood and sex. I dragged the first guy I could get my hands on back to my room and fucked his brains out. It was a feeding frenzy topped with toe-curling, boneless, leg-shaking sex."

Abigail blinked at her. "You can't be serious. You're dating Gehrig. His Were blood should slake your thirst for months. Plus, Weres satiate other appetites better than most, so what the hell?"

"I know! That's what's so crazy disturbing." She exhaled. "Anyway, Rémy sensed the underlying peculiarity well. Or at least I think he noted the telltale lure. Maybe he's old enough to handle whatever sent me into a sexual feeding frenzy. Or maybe he's just old."

Abigail shut her laptop and grabbed her office keys. "Vampires don't exhaust donors to the point of expiring. Bleed them dry, sure, but we don't sex them to death. There's only two supernatural entities that do that, and neither are allowed into the Red Veil without clearing permission through me."

"You're not listening, Abby. The donor was drained. Every ounce. Yet this unusual scent wasn't on him. It was as if someone released an airborne drug that robs the undead of their senses."

"Don't be daft."

The clock on the wall chimed loudly as Abigail locked up her desk. "Where is Rémy now?"

"I'm here." Rémy stood in the doorway to Abigail's office. "I didn't want to waste time, so if the mountain won't come to Mohammed —"

"Rémy." Abigail put her keys down. "I was on my way. Bette was filling me in on what happened."

His frown deepened. "Did you call Dash?"

"No." She glanced at Bette. "Other than being drained, do we know who the victim was or what precipitated his death?" Abby asked.

Rémy moved to a chair in front of Abigail's desk and sat, shaking his head. "The victim was a Were, which complicates matters in the extreme."

"We'll need as much information as possible," Abigail added. "The Alpha of the Brethren and his hunters will want answers."

"I know." Rémy agreed. "We'll have no choice but to tell them eventually. Sean Leighton has every right to demand such. If the situation was reversed, we certainly would, though I would rather wait until we know more."

"I'll tell you what I think," Bette interrupted. "I think an outsider gained access to the backrooms without consent. I think they somehow found and manipulated the worst of our kind. Vampire dregs.

"Maybe one of the forbidden entities, like a demon or an incubus are responsible. From the look of what was left of that poor soul, whoever or whatever was responsible allowed the vampires involved to feed very well. Viciously well."

Abby shook her head again. "We have wards for that very reason. No one could get through."

"If the culprit is none of the above, then who?" Bette asked.

Rémy templed his fingers, his face like stone. "It was neither a demon nor an incubus. It was an entity we never anticipated."

"Why would you say that? Rémy, what do you know?" Abigail asked, stunned.

"My gut tells me it was a *Cinn ag Taitneamh*."

Bette looked from one to the other. "Wait, a Sin Egg Tat…what?" "

Abigail stood stunned, ignoring Bette.

He nodded, his expression tightening. "It's Gaelic, Bette. "Loosely translated, it means Shining Ones."

"Sidhe. Fae devils." Abigail sank back into her chair.

Rémy nodded again. "Yes, and if memory serves, it's not good. The Unseelie are powerful and innately magical. Malevolent, when it suits them."

Bette swiveled in her chair to face Rémy. "Are you telling us a Dark Fae killed a Were in our backrooms? How? If we have wards for other forbidden entities, how did we let this slippery sucker get through?"

"Good question," he acknowledged. "And one we need to answer sooner than later. An incubus, or a succubus or even a demon would have doubtless set off our wards. But this—" Rémy shook his head. "Someone invited this dark Sidhe into our world. There's no other explanation that fits."

Bette pursed her lips, unsure. "Wait. I thought the undead were the only supernaturals that needed an invitation to enter a private space."

"I don't mean that kind of invitation, Bette. What I mean is indications point to this dark Sidhe having help." He gave Abigail a dubious look. "Inside help."

"Don't look at me," she balked. "I certainly didn't let an Unseelie through our doors."

"No, but you oversee our wards. When was the last time their strength was confirmed?"

Abigail snatched her keys from her blotter and unlocked the top drawer to her desk. "Two days ago."

She pulled a black ledger from the narrow drawer and opened it to the center. Turning the book around, she tapped the latest entry. "I carried out a full test myself. One of the newer sentinels was with me. It's part of their training program."

Rémy leaned forward to look at the logbook, but Bette caught Abby's eye, still confused.

"I thought the Fae only messed with humans, and then only when it suited them. What could they possibly gain coming here?"

"Dark Sidhe are caprice incarnate," Rémy replied, closing the book. "This could've been nothing more than sport, but when they crossed into our backrooms, they violated our sanctuary. Even the Sidhe know a vampire's lair is sacrosanct." He pushed the log back to Abigail. "Your records are impeccable as always. I apologize for jumping to the wrong conclusion."

She nodded once, but Rémy's sudden backdoor accusation left her nonplussed. Abby was old school, and would never question a master elder, but her eyes were daggers.

"Abigail." Rémy considered the tight set of her jaw. "We are creatures who live on a divided precipice. Ruled both by reason and by desire. Put yourself in my shoes. You would have considered the outside possibility as well, however upsetting. We are, after all, dealing with a Sidhe." He shrugged, unapologetic. "Occam's Razor."

"I don't understand." Bette bristled. "What does the Tinkerbell Club have to do with accusing one of our own?"

Rémy ignored the question. "You employ youngbloods as sentinels, yes?" he asked Abigail.

"It's been our policy for a while," she replied. "We've found their residual human blood makes it easy for them to blend with the crowds at the club. The fact they're also the strongest and most biddable of our kind makes them the perfect counterpart to the Were guard dogs we traditionally employ. Of course, once their lingering human blood dissipates, we dismiss them."

"Interesting."

Abby cocked her head. "The elders never concerned themselves with the details of running the club. At least Sebastién never did. What do my youngbloods have to do with any of this?"

Bette's mouth dropped, and her eyes jerked to Rémy. "Are you saying you think youngbloods made some sort of deal with a Fae?"

Abby's large office suddenly seemed small. Rémy reached for the desk phone and made a quick call, and when he hung up, he turned toward both sets of questioning eyes.

"I can't answer your question, Bette, because I no longer know." He shook his head. "I'm positive a Sidhe was responsible for what happened to this

unfortunate shifter. What we need to find out is if they had help from a few traitorous youngbloods, and whether or not that help was compulsion or a pact."

Abigail sat in considered silence, sparing a glance for Bette. "I can't believe this was consciously done."

"Again, Occam's Razor. Until proven otherwise, we have to investigate."

"Well, sitting like three undead bumps on a log doesn't help anything. What do we do now?" Bette asked.

The clocked ticked in the background, making the tension seem worse. "We call the council," Rémy replied. "We can't handle this alone."

"Wait a minute." Bette raised an eyebrow. "We handle every other supernatural entity that crosses our threshold. Why not these puffed up pixies? Is there something you two senior citizens aren't saying? If I know Rémy, there's a history lesson in here somewhere."

He cracked a smile. "Since you asked so nicely, I'll tell you. With the help of the Druids, the Sidhe nearly enslaved our kind five millennia ago. Fae blood is both an aphrodisiac and addictive to vampires. It's very, very hard to resist. A thousand times more addicting to us than our blood is to the Weres. One taste and we are at their mercy."

"So, your guess about our youngbloods makes sense."

He nodded. "Unfortunately, yes."

She considered Rémy's words, but then swung her eyes to Abigail. "That unusual scent. It has got to be a telltale sign. Maybe it's a clue that'll help us get to the bottom of how this happened."

Rémy looked between them. "What scent?"

Abigail opened her mouth, but Bette beat her to it. "You were standing right next to me in the room, Rémy. Are you saying you didn't smell that sweet, underlying sexual current? It should have made the hair on your arms stand up, dude." She glanced to his crotch and then back again. "Among other things."

"Classy, Bette."

The younger vampire blew out a breath. "I'm sorry. Whatever lingered in that room was an unequivocal turn on, okay? The effect it had on me was unlike anything I ever experienced. I was so frenzied I did what was necessary to find release."

"An airborne aphrodisiac," Abby explained, giving Rémy an apologetic look. "

Rémy lifted an eyebrow. "If lingering magic had that kind of effect on Bette, imagine what actual Fae blood did to those youngbloods."

"Why weren't you affected?" Bette asked, curious. "Is that due to vampiric age? Because if

that's the case, I'll stay a youngblood forever, thank you very much."

He let his eyes drift from Bette's eyes to her breasts and back again. "What makes you so certain I wasn't affected? Perhaps quick release is the only option for those less experienced."

Rémy stifled a chuckle at the look on Bette's face. "We senior citizens can take our time and savor the moment."

"All righty, then. On that note…" Abigail pressed the intercom. "Calypso, I need a list of who from the vampire staff is unaccounted for this evening."

Rémy nodded. "Good start. I'll summon the remaining council. One of us will have to contact the Alpha of the Brethren once we gather our information."

Abby's phone dinged with a text message, and she glanced at the screen. "Dash is meeting with Sean today. He says the meeting should go well into the night."

"That buys us a little time. We'll reconvene in my quarters in an hour. My gut tells me that poor Were is just the beginning."

Chapter Six

*O*il-stained torches lit the way, giving the setting a medieval feel. Their footsteps echoed on the stone tile, the staccato rhythm mingling with the sounds of pleasure and pain drifting in from various rooms.

Gareth's body language ignored the pleasant and not so pleasant, but a sharp yelp jerked his head toward the loudest of them.

His grip tightened on her hand, and a strong protective air enveloped her like a warm blanket. There was a time she hoped for that kind of consistency and strength in a relationship. A love to last the ages. Deep down she still did, despite every attempt to bury what she thought was lost.

Of course, now that Gareth was back—

You hope.

That one word scared her more than any rogue Sidhe ever could. She pushed the feeling away and concentrated instead on Gareth's wide shoulders and the way his muscled torso narrowed toward the gorgeous curve of his ass. Sex was something she understood. Primal. No thought required.

Hope.

Stop that.

Okay, how about hoping he's still as good in the sack as ever?

She put the brakes on her runaway emotional roller coaster. Eve, first. Sexy former, yet soon-to-be again lover, later.

She made herself stare at the spot between Gareth's shoulder blades, instead of his strong, muscular legs.

From there she cleared her mind enough to try and sense Eve. This was not a place her friend would have consented to go on her own.

Closing her eyes, she summoned her power. Energy rose, skittering beneath her skin so quickly it startled her. She opened her eyes, expecting the dim corridor to crackle blue with magic, but it was as dark as before, and Gareth was still a single pace ahead.

Their hands were linked, and when she concentrated on their laced fingers, energy flowed in a clear conduit. He had combined his power with hers again, giving her strength and solidarity.

If she could've kissed him then she would, but they had derailed themselves enough already.

Confident, she dove deeper, bringing their joined power to a head. The merger showed her glimpses from Gareth's mind. Images rushed forward. Pain he suffered. Death he suffered. She

was about to sever the bond when she saw herself as he remembered…her face flushed with need…their bodies wrapped as her thighs shook…him gripping her hips, thrust after thrust.

Her panties dampened at the X-rated memories.

Would it be the same, now?

She imagined how he'd tease her, inch by inch, holding back just enough to make her beg.

"What's that, love? I can't hear you." His breathy whisper making her nipples ache for his tongue. *"You want this?"* Him, fisting his cock, its corded length taut between her slick folds. *"Hard and deep or slow and torturous?"* Inch by inch, he'd tantalize, keeping her arms locked and her legs spread until she was ready to burst.

Fuck. She stifled a gasp. So much for derailing their mission. Lane took a breath to get a grip, only to hear him chuckle.

"Cut it out, Gareth," she ground out.

He glanced over his shoulder. "What? I'm just walking here."

"Give it a rest, Robert DeNiro. Put a lid on Memory Lane. I can't focus."

"Really."

"Gareth!"

He chuckled again. "That last one was all you, love. In fact, I'm having a moment myself. You certainly know how to put the F in fantasy. I'll never look at neckties the same way."

A self-satisfied grin tugged at her lips. "*Ties that bind* is more than just an old saying, and possibly something we should explore—later."

He groaned, squaring his shoulders. "You're killing me, Smalls."

Her heart squeezed at the movie quote. Memory flashed again, and she smiled at the sweet recollection. The two had broken Caitlan's curfew, sneaking downstairs to watch *The Sandlot* on a DVD player in the janitor's storage room. Cuddled up in a blanket, it was the first time they kissed. The first time they…and Gareth remembered.

"Can you sense her?"

"Her?" Lane coughed, startled from her musing.

"Eve. Remember?"

She shook off what was left of her reverie and called their shared power again. They were deep into the blood-play zone. This time Eve's trace hit full and in her face.

"She's here, or at least she was."

They stopped, and Lane turned toward a series of doors along the corridor. One by one she moved past each, holding that single thought like a divining staff.

The moans were loud, but most of the doors were either locked or warded. She hesitated at the last, stopping with her hand over the knob.

"Wait. I should go first," he said, moving her to the side before she could grab hold.

She wasn't about to argue.

The knob turned easily enough, and Gareth pushed it wide without hesitation.

"Anything?" she asked, craning to see around him.

"Plenty, but it's not what we hoped."

Lane pushed past him but stopped short just inside the room. "Oh, goddess. No."

Tied to a large, merry-go-round style platform was the shifter Eve had spelled at the bar.

"Mason." Her voice was a whisper as she walked toward the prone Were.

"You know this guy?"

She nodded slowly. "He was with Eve on the dance floor before I lost sight of them."

The round apparatus had no grab bars, just leather restraints at strategic points. The unfortunate Were was bound wrists and ankles, like Leonardo da Vinci's *Vitruvian Man*. His body was covered in torn flesh and random bitemarks.

Gareth moved to the platform's edge, reaching to check the man for a pulse. He looked up, meeting Lane's eyes before shaking his head.

He straightened from the shifter's lifeless form, the movement rotating the platform a few inches.

Gareth spared a look for Lane before bending to rock the platform back and forth. "Fucking thing

spins, like a carnival wheel. They played goddamned spin the bottle with him." He kicked the wooden edge. "Fucking leeches made a game out of a gang feeding! Bastards!"

A single chair with silk fetters sat directly across from the rotating platform. Lane moved toward it, lifting one of the silken ties in her hand.

"They tied Eve to the chair, making her watch as Mason begged for his life." Lane winced, images flooding as her fingers twisted the silk.

"You have a choice, darling girl. Submit or your friend dies."

The Sidhe's hands clutched Eve's shoulders. Covetous and greedy. He wanted her, but she wasn't the prize.

"Where's your friend? I had hoped the idea of a threesome would be appealing. She frequents these hallowed halls enough, I thought she'd be game," he taunted, nipping her ear. "I could make you fetch her."

Eve's nipples hardened and he laughed. His hands hadn't moved from her shoulders, but her clit throbbed and with a single word, she came hard, crying out in her restraints.

"We can do this all night, my dear. I want Lane Alden. My raven will come home to roost, if I have to kidnap every member of your precious circle. Your supreme eluded me when I wanted her, but this time I will have my quarry."

Lane's hand went to her stomach and she doubled over, retching on the floor.

"What happened?" Gareth rushed to her side, ripping the silk from her hand, breaking the vision.

"There were three vampires, and they were all in some kind of thrall." She dragged in a breath before meeting Gareth's eyes. "Leith isn't kidnapping Fae-kissed witches to regain anything. He's looking for me. He wants me."

Gareth hesitated before nodding. "I know."

Straightening slowly, she wiped the back of her hand across her mouth. "What do you mean, you know?"

He waited, almost as if measuring his words. "I was sent."

"Sent? By whom?"

He pulled his hand back from between her shoulder blades. "Does it matter? I failed. Leith has Eve, and now you won't stop until you find her."

"Of course, it matters." She took a step toward him. "Gareth, please. Since I'm the one he wants, I think I deserve to know."

He exhaled, lifting a hand to his forehead. "Ten years has passed since you watched me burn, but for me it's been no more than a year. No more than that since the Unseelie untied me from the pyre in the motherhouse courtyard, waiting for me to rise from the ash. They burned me in our own

backyard, laughing from a distance as they watched you and the others try to save me."

"I was there, remember. We were too late." She paused. "I was too late."

"You were spelled, Laney. You all were. They used a power the Seelie queen is still trying to decipher. All we know is it requires blood. Witch's blood." His eyes met hers. "Raven blood."

"Eve."

He didn't reply.

"How would they even know she's Fae-kissed? She hasn't completed her initiation."

Gareth looked at her. "They know. Almost as if they can smell the latency. They tried and lost with me, so taking a novice is the next logical step. The truth is, they can control a witch that hasn't fully come into her power, and a Fae-kissed Raven is even more of a prize.

"When they took me, they thought they captured a weapon. A rare Phoenix Fae, albeit a half-breed. One they could keep and bleed for their own purposes. What they didn't expect was me taking an iron sword to their throats three days later, giving it back to them three times over."

Lane's heart squeezed at the remembered visions she glimpsed. "Three times three. You have nothing to regret. You followed our rules. Whatever you put out, comes back threefold."

"Leave it to you to find poetic justice, courtesy of our Wiccan Rede." His eyes flicked to the platform again. "We need to find Eve before it's too late."

"We?" she asked. "You still haven't said how you know about all this. By your own admission you said you were in Faerie."

Gareth's eyes took on a gold hue, and Lane gasped, taking a step back. "You really are a Fae. Is there even any witch left?"

"I'm still very much a witch." He exhaled, shrugging. "I'm a half-breed, like you, but I've found acceptance and purpose in the Seelie Court. Light Sidhe can be capricious and impolitic, same as their dark Sidhe counterparts. They are quick to take offense and retaliate when given reason, unlike the Unseelie who are cruel for sport.

"The Seelie queen is kind and does her best to be just. Well, as much as a Fae can be. There's a tentative truce between the two courts. A common enemy will do that. Just look at the Vampires and Weres since the HepZ outbreak."

"You know about that?" Stunned, she looked at him.

"There's little we don't hear about. You forget, Faerie mirrors the mortal plane."

She snorted. "I don't believe that for a second. Soot, grit, smog. I don't think so. The only things

we share are greed, ambition, and debauchery." She spared a pained glance for Mason.

He lifted his fingers to her cheek. "What about me? Do you believe me?"

The simple touch opened another cascade of memories and how Gareth was everything to her —

Once upon a time.

The way he looked now, with his lips parted, she angled her head to match his, primed for a kiss. She covered his hand, the urge to crush her mouth to his almost too much.

He pulled away slowly. Lane didn't fight him or say anything. Not because she had no words, but because she didn't trust herself.

"So, Golden Boy, how are we going to locate Eve?"

"Golden Boy?"

He was right. This was no time for humor.

"Sorry, Gareth. If you've found something that works to help you heal, then who am I to poke fun? Maybe I'm jealous, but that doesn't excuse the fact this entire situation is all my fault." Her regret was clear, and she glanced at her feet.

"No, Laney. This goes way beyond you. You saw the three vampires when you read the residual energy. Leith had help. From the inside. Both courts suspected as much. Why else would I be here? In this club?"

At that, her head jerked up. "Wait, vampires are working both sides?"

"Not exactly. But it explains why your shifter friend looks like a chew toy. It's all about the blood, Lane. Nothing works in this club without it."

"It's a vampire club, Gareth. Not exactly a trade secret. Despite the fact our blood doesn't do the trick." She lifted a hand. "Present company excluded, obviously."

"That's a fallacy. Witch blood may be poisonous to vampires, but the Fae trace in ours counteracts that anomaly. You saw the effects for yourself with the vampire at the entrance. Fae blood in its purest form is more than a temptation for the undead. It's addictive, the same way vampire blood is addicting to Weres."

She shook her head. "Not always. I know vampires and Weres who share blood and more, if you know what I mean. They consider themselves mates, and they're perfectly fine."

"Weres and shifters don't need blood for sustenance. Plus, they're basically human, despite their dual natures, and can choose moderation. Vampires don't discriminate when it comes to blood wants and needs. So, if a willing donor happens to be even more adept at manipulation than the undead feeding from their vein?"

"Like a dark Sidhe."

He nodded.

She wasn't convinced. "If our blood is safe, and our Fae trace so alluring, then how come we're not swarmed by trolling undead as if we're their next meal?"

"Two answers. One. Glamour. Two. The truth about Raven blood is a very well-kept secret. Purposefully well kept."

"This sucks." She exhaled, puffing her breath out in an agitated rush. "Pun totally intended."

"I agree."

Lane crossed her arms, scanning the mayhem once more. "So, what's our next move?" She hesitated, eyeing Mason's prone body.

"What is it? What do you see?"

Lifting a staying hand, she walked toward the platform and bent over the restraint holding Mason's right wrist.

"Well, well, well." She reached for the dead Were's clenched fist, and untangled a few strands of long, yellow hair from his fingers. "I think our unfortunate friend might not have died in vain." She held the glimmering strands to the light and smiled. "Bingo."

"You can't scry for a Sidhe, Laney. They don't respond to summonses."

She grinned. "Who said anything about a summoning? I'm thinking we use it to crush the bastard, but first we need bait."

"Oh, no you don't. The first thing we need to do is get you to get to the motherhouse. Caitlan will have the place warded better than Faerie itself. I'll take things from there."

"Not a chance." She met his blue-eyed gaze head on. "There's a dead Were in the backrooms of the Red Veil, courtesy of a dark Sidhe and his vampire minions. The bastard made it clear he wants me, so what better way to catch him than tempting him with what he wants?"

"Lane, no."

She wasn't taking no for an answer. "Look, I'm not suggesting I sit naked on a Faerie mound covered in laurels. We need a plan, and yes, that means Caitlan and the motherhouse library. If anyone knows why this Sidhe-tard wants me, it's got to be Caitlan, or at the very least she'll know where to look for the answer."

Lane moved toe-to-toe with Gareth, going up on the balls of her feet to press a kiss to his lips. "Think of how surprised she'll be when we show up together."

Yeah, right. Just like old times.

Chapter Seven

*L*ane's footsteps echoed in time with Gareth's along the cracked sidewalks. The city slowed its pulse in the hours before daybreak, the near quiet unnerving. Especially when you knew what might lurk in the shadows.

The motherhouse wasn't far, but at this time of night even a short distance seemed to take forever. A fixture in lower Manhattan, the motherhouse watched in serene detachment as history molded and remolded the surrounding city.

The house itself was an anomaly, a hidden treasure in plain sight amid diverse neighborhoods. Still, remnants of bygone days were evidenced in the cobbled streets that ran side-by-side with asphalt and rebar. Harkening back to the history that brought the witches to the New World.

"A half hour ago, you chirped with ideas. Why so quiet now?" Gareth asked, sneaking a look at Lane as they crossed the street.

"I'm preparing myself for battle."

"Good." He nodded in reply. "Forearmed is best. Especially when you already anticipate the worst."

Lane slid a glance his way. "I can't tell if you're being straight or snarky."

Gareth chuckled. "Both."

"Gee, thanks," she retorted, linking her arm with his. "You're the one the Sidhe royals sent as reinforcement. I should be confident, not worried."

"Now who's being snarky?" He chuckled again, but slowed their pace, his muscles tightening beneath Lane's hold. "Caitlan did a good job. I can feel her wards from here."

"Par for the course. Her protective vibe has been on overdrive for months. I wonder if she has had premonitions about this all along." Lane indicated the rich brownstone nestled inside a small fenced yard. "Home sweet home. The old girl hasn't changed that much since you left."

"No," he replied, taking in the elegant façade. "I'm surprised some developer hasn't bribed City Hall to press for eminent domain to put up some glass and steel monstrosity."

Lane pressed the intercom on the outer gate. "I meant Caitlan, but you're right about the real estate rats. They sic their lawyers and pocket politicos on us from time to time, but like you said, Caity Cat's wards are very good." She winked.

The gate slid seamlessly into its sheath within the decorative front stone wall. "In case you hadn't noticed, the gate and the entire perimeter are wrought iron."

Lane held out a hand, her delicate silver bracelets tinkling on her wrist. "Caitlan did that…after." She gave him a quick smile. "Anyway, the iron is by design. She wanted to ensure we never had a repeat of what happened with you."

"You can't put loved ones in a magic bubble, Laney. If someone is intent on harm, they find a way." He took her hand, kissing it before folding it with his. "Still, I can't blame her for trying."

The slate walk shimmered as they made their way to the front door. They climbed the wide stairs in awkward silence and stood on the porch.

"You ready?" she asked.

Gareth touched the raven-shaped doorknocker in reply, and the stained glass framing the sigil glowed.

"The house remembers you, Gareth."

He smiled. "I half expected Caitlan to imbue all kinds of cosmic nasties in case I went over to the dark side."

"If she did, the cosmic karma would be for me, not for you. She knows how much I like cookies."

He raised an eyebrow. "Cookies?"

"The meme? Come to the dark side. We have cookies?" She curled her fingers, teasing.

"Nope."

"I guess Faerie doesn't keep up with as much as they think."

He smirked in reply, watching her press her hand to the front door. "Witchy biometrics?"

The door lock clicked open, and she reached for the knob. "Layered spell work, but basically the same premise. Except ours makes the trespasser wish he'd never been born."

"I'll keep that in mind," he replied, but then hesitated as she turned the door handle. "Are you sure about this, Laney? I'm prepared to handle Leith on my own."

"This goes deeper than making a rogue Sidhe my bitch. I need to know my history, Gareth. Maybe that will explain why this happened in the first place. Whoever Leith is to me or to you, or whatever his relationship to either court, the truth needs outing. For Eve, but also for Mason. My gut tells me he was an innocent that got caught up in something he didn't understand."

"Okay. I know you've got skills, and that Caitlan has your back, but this is not going to be an easy fight."

The sobering thought forced her to glance at the street, and how different things were twelve hours ago when she and Eve set out for their night on the town.

The front door creaked open, pulling Lane's attention from the street. A woman with long silvery-pink hair stood in the doorway, her large blue eyes sweeping Gareth before she uttered a single word.

"So, the prodigal returns." The large onyx stone on her index finger winked in the hall light.

"Caitlan." Gareth flashed a close-lipped grin. "As welcoming as ever. Though I didn't expect you'd greet us yourself."

Her aqua eyes gave nothing away. "It's the least I could do, considering how forthcoming you've been over the years."

"And she's back," he replied with a short sigh.

Lane frowned at them both. "Give it a rest, both of you. Caitlan, you're as happy to see Gareth as I am, so cut it out. We were all traumatized by what happened ten years ago, Gareth especially, since he's the one that burned at the stake. I'm sure he has a long and interesting explanation for how he survived, and why he thought it best to keep that fact a secret, but right now we have bigger Fae to fry."

Neither said anything in reply, and Lane met Caitlan's considering stare, despite the awkward silence.

Lane exchanged an uncertain glance with Gareth. "Okay then. I'll take your no comment as a yes."

She took a step toward Caitlan, still blocking the entry. "Are you planning to let us in, or should Gareth and I strategize from a hotel room somewhere?"

Their Supreme stepped to the side, the motion an acknowledgment of the situation, not an absolution.

"Gareth, I had your old room prepared," she replied, closing the door behind them. "I'm sure you can remember the way."

Lane spared her quizzical look. "I didn't tell you we were coming."

"And I didn't bake a cake, so we're even," Caitlan answered with a dismissive wave.

"How-ja do. How-ja do."

Caitlan flashed him soft grin.

"Okay, then. I'm sure that's a private joke of sorts, and one I haven't a clue about, but it only proves me right. You are happy to see Gareth, so cut it with the wicked witch stuff."

Caitlan considered the younger witch, giving her a half smile. "It's not a private joke, it's a hit song from the 1950s...*If I knew you were coming, I'd have baked a cake*...but I am guilty as charged. I'm glad you're both home, though I am a little insulted you doubted my powers of precognition."

She sighed, letting her gaze fall on Gareth again. "It's good to have you home, little frog, but don't

think for one second you're excused from giving me a detailed accounting."

"Little frog?" Lane raised an eyebrow.

"Long story. Don't ask."

Caitlan winked at Gareth's quick blush, but then sobered again. "You two can play twenty questions once this dirty business is put to bed. My guess is you'll need our library, though I'm afraid you're on your own. We all are, as I've sent the rest of the initiates into seclusion. I will answer what I can, but without our archivist, I can't promise much."

"What happened to Grania?" Gareth asked. "Is she still full of piss and vinegar? I remember thinking she was so pickled sour, she'd live forever."

Sadness creased Caitlan's face, and Lane elbowed Gareth's side. "I'm sorry, Gareth. She died quite suddenly, last year. Caro has taken over, but a history like ours takes time."

Caitlan turned her eyes toward the stairs. "Go on up, then. Most of your belongings were put into storage, but I managed a pair of sweats and an old tee from a trunk I kept. They've been washed and folded and are on the bed in your room. I'll see the clothes you're wearing are washed and returned by morning."

She looked at Lane. "In the meantime, there are bottles of water and cookies on a tray in the hall.

Take what you want and then meet me in the library in an hour. I'll brew a pot of coffee and scrounge up some real food."

They watched the willowy woman head toward the kitchen at the back of the house.

"I told you the dark side had cookies."

Gareth nodded absently. "With Caitlan, I believe it."

"Still, that went better than I expected." Lane turned with him toward the stairs.

"Is it me or did Caitlan seem a little too prepared for us? Do you think she knows more than what we anticipated?"

"Your guess is as good as mine, *little frog*," Lane teased.

"*Ribbit.* And no, I'm not telling you how I got the nickname. Let's just say the transfiguration scene in *Harry Potter* has nothing on Caitlan when she wants to make a point."

"She didn't! Why didn't you ever tell me?"

Gareth opened his mouth to reply, but something at the top of the stairs caught his eye. "I thought Caitlan said we were on our own."

"She did."

How many Ravens are in residence right now?"

"Nine, including me and Eve."

Gareth looked from the empty landing to where Lane stood at the bottom step. "A full coven."

"Twelve's better, but we do okay. Of course, most residents are initiates from all over. Only Eve and one other girl are true Ravens. Why?"

They climbed the stairs, past framed herbs and pressed magical plants. "Just curious."

Lane stepped onto the top landing first, pivoting toward a set of private doors off the second-floor hallway. Gareth followed, and the two stopped in front of a plain door where she waited for him to say something.

"Well, at least there's no skull and crossbones on the center panel."

Lane stepped to the side, giving Gareth the honors. "Believe it or not, she kept it as is for years. She only agreed to clean it out when the dust mites threatened a coup."

He cracked a grin, turning the knob. The door swung open and he stood for a moment staring at the dim interior. "Wow. Caitlan wasn't kidding," he murmured.

Lane slipped past to snap on the light. The room was immaculate, smelling of lemon polish and beeswax. Two wide pillar candles flickered from the dresser and the nightstand, bathing everything in soft light.

Gareth caught Lane's eye in the dresser mirror. "Feels like old times, huh."

"Wickedly so." She absently wrapped a hand over the smooth bedpost attached to the footboard.

"Wicked?"

A nostalgic grin tugged at her lips. "After what we did in here, right under Caitlan's twitchy nose?" She shrugged off a soft chuckle. "We'd have to be as naïve as we were then to assume she still doesn't know."

Gareth closed the door. "Are you talking about then or now?"

Without waiting for her to answer, he crossed the width of the room, moving in until the back of Lane's thighs pressed tight to the polished wood.

"You're as beautiful as I remember, Laney. Soft and luminous. With a mouth that begs kissing."

She met his blue eyes glittering in the candlelight. "We were so young."

"We were." He cupped both of her cheeks, letting his thumb trace the edge of her bottom lip. "But that doesn't mean we didn't have something real. We've come full circle, Lane. You and me. You bewitched me then, and you bewitch me now."

His thumb stopped its caress, and he held her chin as his eyes searched her steady gaze. "You know what I want, and I know you want it, too."

Her single word was all Gareth needed. He leaned in, taking her mouth. She moaned against his lips, and in seconds his hand slipped to the nape of her neck, urging more. Demanding more.

Breath mingled, hands tangled in hair, their tongues fought and plundered, hungry and exacting.

Gareth's hand slid to skim to her collarbone, trailing lower to tease the swell of one breast.

The candles were a dead giveaway their Supreme predicted this moment, despite her reserve at the door. Orchestrated it even. That Caitlan set the stage for a witchy booty call left her cheeks burning almost as much as Gareth's kiss.

Breathless, she broke their kiss with her hands still twisted in his dark hair. "Gareth—"

"You are so beautiful, Lane. Even more so when you're too stubborn to admit you're horny."

He shook his head, lifting a finger to her lips "Your eyes are wide and dilated, and your lips slightly swollen. Your cheeks flushed. If I slipped my hand into your panties, my fingers would find you warm and slick."

"Gareth," she tried again, only to be silenced with another kiss.

She put her hands on his shoulders and pushed him back one step. Keeping her palm on his chest, she kept him at arm's length.

"What are you doing?" he asked, watching her loose the knit tieback from one of her belle sleeves.

Dangling it between them, a teasing smirk curved on her lips. "Remember?"

"You are such a tease. Fearless and sexy, but definitely a tease." He took the tieback from her hand and pulled its mate loose from her other sleeve.

"I'm going to take these as a yes," he said, holding the tiebacks in his palm, "but I still want to hear you say the word. You know how I feel, and I've made it very clear what I want."

"Graphically clear."

He waited, toying with the black knit ties. "Not good enough."

"The bedposts await, my lord." Lane bowed her head, lifting both wrists toward him.

Chapter Eight

Gareth held her chin, lifting her face. "What did you say, Lane?"

A soft gasp muffled the word as he cupped her breast through her blouse, giving her nipple a pinch.

"I'm sorry, what was that?" he teased.

"Please," she croaked.

"Please what?"

She licked her lips. This game made her clit throb and her pussy so wet, the slick warmth drenched her panties. Same as it did a decade ago, only more now that she'd been in the backrooms. If they ever settled this mess with the Sidhe Courts, she had a particular room she'd love to show Gareth.

"I'm waiting," he said, letting his thumb roll her taut bud again.

She sucked in a breath. "Fuck me, Gareth! Fuck me boneless so I come like rockets!"

He separated her from her blouse, lifting it over her head and tossing the sheer material to the floor beside the bed. Holding her wrists high, he

unbuttoned her pants, releasing her hands only to push the pants to the floor, along with her lace undies.

"Mmmm," he smirked, letting his fingers graze her slick sex as he dragged his hand back to her waist.

Skimming even higher, he cupped her breasts again, only this time he pulled her bralette down to push her nipples up and over the edge of the lace.

"You have beautiful tits, Lane. You always did. So luscious. So inviting." Gareth's hands grazed the taut peaks, letting the bra's straps fall over her shoulders.

"I remember how I'd itch to touch you in class. To run my fingers over your nipples in secret." He dipped his head, flicking one pink peak with his tongue.

Lane inhaled deep, letting her head drop back. "I remember sex in the stacks."

"The library. Magical theory." He dipped his head again. "How many books did we knock off those shelves, rolling around in the dust?"

Her breath came in short pants, and she didn't answer. Instead, she cupped both breasts, arching them further to his mouth.

"Those books were as hard as my cock is right now." He bit down, grazing her sensitive flesh. "I'm so hard I could drill diamonds with the tip of

my cock, but the only thing I'm going to drill is your pretty pink pussy."

The candlelight shimmered on her pale skin, and he took a step back, his gaze burning as it traveled her full length.

"Sit." He motioned to the edge of the bed. "Spread your legs."

"Wouldn't you rather me—"

He reached for her breast again, giving her nipple a hard pinch. She gasped at the mix of pleasure and pain. To follow delicious orders was a release from the day-to-day, knowing full well she could turn the tables on Gareth any time. And she would.

Her clit jerked at the thought of him on his knees, her hands in his hair and his gorgeous, talented mouth between her slick folds. Two could play at this, and she would keep her dominant side in check for the time being.

She slid onto the mattress, and as he pulled her toward the edge, her sensitive mound brushed the hard bar beneath his fly.

Her breath hitched at the rough feel of his fingers when he dipped a hand to her wet sex, his mouth to one nipple, drawing the stiff bud between his teeth.

Circling the puckered flesh, he teased and sucked, rolling the other between his fingers.

"Your pussy is so ripe, you're ready to burst. But I'm going to make you sweat for it. It's been ten years, so what's a few more minutes?"

Lane's fingers clutched the bedspread, but he didn't relent. She sucked in a breath as he worked the slick folds between her legs. He fisted her pussy, his fingers curling deep and punishing. She moaned, arching her hips to grind his hand closer to her clit.

"Not so fast, love," he murmured. Holding both her wrists in one hand, he pulled his other from her slick slit and pointed to the headboard.

Her skin was on fire, and her body hummed with need as she scooted backwards toward the pillows, watching him lick her essence from his fingers.

Scooping her knit tiebacks from the duvet, he walked around the side of the bed to the bedpost nearest the pillows.

"Do you remember our safe word?" she asked.

Their gazes locked, and he lifted her wrist to the post. "Fire." He bound her wrist tight before doing the same with the other on the opposite side.

Wispy feathers and silk flowers stood in a decorative vase on a side table. Gareth reached for a delicate plume and placed it on one of the pillows.

Lane watched, licking her lips as he stripped out of his clothes, grinning to herself when he pulled a clean handkerchief from his pocket.

"That for me?" she said, letting her lips slide into a smirk.

"Sexual sensory overload," he murmured, tying the handkerchief blindfold style over her eyes.

She felt weight shift on the bed, and then heard footsteps before the sound of running water.

"Gareth?" she called after him, lifting her head to try and see out the bottom edge.

When he came back, she felt the mattress dip again, and his clean, masculine scent, close enough to make her mouth water.

He spread her knees wide, circling her clit with his thumb. "You're already dripping, but I want to see what you do when something even hotter hits your spot."

He got up again, and this time when he came back, she heard a plastic cap snap open. She sucked in a breath as something very hot, but very silky, trickled over her belly and between her legs.

Gareth's hands smoothed the steamy lube, teasing her clit and folds. Her skin immediately tingled hot and cold, the feeling incredible and electric.

She gasped, the sensation aching for friction. Lifting her hips, he answered with something steaming and rough.

With a sharp intake, she bucked higher, but he held her off, letting the course edge of something rough and wet graze her flesh.

Panting for contact, her hands struggled against her restraints. "*Argh*. Gareth! What is that? I want it. Please! Give me something! My body is burning!"

"Amazing what a hot, damp hand towel can do." He chuckled. "How about a little of this?"

Lifting the feather from the vase, he trailed it over her taut nipples, teasing her again with the ghost of a touch.

She squirmed against the slow, sexy torment. He dipped his mouth to her lips, letting his tongue spar with hers, taking her higher and higher, but left her body screaming for touch and release.

Lane groaned against his mouth, her breasts aching for his mouth and his hands. "You suck, Gareth!" She gritted her teeth and arched her back.

"All you had to do was ask, love." He chuckled, dropping his head to her nipples, his tongue rasping and licking, sucking, and biting.

Slipping his hand to her pussy, he teased her wet slit with a single finger. Tracing the outline of her folds until she growled.

"Damn you, Gareth! Fuck ME!"

"You know, Caitlin never found our stash. Picture my surprise when I checked under the loose bathroom tile and found our bag of tricks. It was as well-hidden and well-preserved as if it was yesterday. Imagine how pissed she'd be if she knew

we vacuum sealed sex toys with her foodsaver back in the day."

Lane felt his weight shift to the edge of the bed and when it evened out, he slipped something over each foot and then up her legs to the juncture between her thighs.

"Remember this?" Her clit jumped as current vibrated against her hard nub. "Madame Butterfly a la Silver Bullet. Ecstasy via remote control."

Electric jolts pulsed through her core and she cried out, lifting her hips. "I took the batteries from your TV clicker. I figured you wouldn't mind." He climbed over, straddling her waist.

"I called you butterfly for weeks, and your clit jumped every time I said the word."

Her mouth dropped open, and he pressed his cock to her lips. "Suck me now, butterfly. Ride the bullet and suck me deep."

With enough slack to lift her head, she licked his engorged head, circling its hard, ridged rim. She sucked him deep, flattening her tongue to milk his corded underside.

"God in heaven!" He drew a sharp breath. "Watching you suck my dick is so fucking hot! That's it, baby, more. Deeper."

He pulled the blindfold from her eyes, and he backed his cock from her lips. Holding the butterfly remote in one hand and his long, thick cock in the

other, he watched her face as he pressed the remote again.

The pulses sharpened in intensity and then backed off to barely a whispered touch. The alternating vibration made her grit her teeth, crying out.

"What? You want to come?" He clicked his cheek. "Sorry, love, but I don't think you're there yet."

He lifted the candle from the nightstand and dripped a small amount of wax over her lower belly.

She hissed, arching her hips. "I want your cock, you bastard!"

"And I want your pussy, slippery and sweet, running wet and slick down my balls as I fuck you."

Gareth slid his hand across her stomach before shifting off her hips. He slid two fingers over her taut core before gliding the same two fingers inside her slick entrance.

Her sex was swollen and ready, and he watched her face as he worked her sex inside and out. His fingers drove deep, while his thumb worked her clit until Lane arched against her restraints, lifting her whole body in delicious agony. She was ready.

"GARETH! If you don't fuck me now, I swear I'll tie you down and ride you 'til your cock turns purple and falls off!"

He pulled his hand back, and she moaned in protest, but he silenced her with an unyielding kiss.

He pulled her knees up and slipped between her thighs, driving his thick length into her with a vicious thrust.

Without missing a beat, he pulled her restraints loose, locking his hands around both her ankles, spreading her wide. His balls smacked against her slick ass as he pounded hard.

She met him trust for thrust, both climbing closer to climax. Eyes blazed, and every muscle contracted, taut and ready. The air shimmered gold around them, same as it did at the Red Veil, only this time it was tangible.

Thick, and suffused with energy, it crackled as though alive. Her blonde hair rose, halo-like, and Gareth gathered her to him, burying himself deeper inside her tight shaft.

Lane's body spasmed, convulsing in delicious release and she cried out. Gareth's eyes glowed gold, and his skin shimmered the same, magical sheen.

Squeezing his eyes shut, he gasped, rigid as his body emptied deep within her. He held tight and taut, and when he finally lifted his lids, his breath locked in his throat.

"Laney, don't look down."

Seeing the stunned look on his face, she did exactly the opposite. "Holy fuck! We're levitating!"

She locked her arms and legs around Gareth's back as they hovered, entwined, five feet above the bed.

"What do we do?" she asked, trying to keep her voice calm.

"Kiss me," he replied. "Kiss me and empty your mind of everything but us and how we feel."

She pressed her mouth to his, letting herself get lost in his taste, his arms, and whoosh! A whirlwind swirled, clearing the air, and they dropped like a stone onto the mattress, breaking the frame with a loud crack.

Still wrapped, they didn't dare move.

"Laney, are you hurt? You okay?" Gareth asked.

Still shaken, she hid her head in the hollow of his throat. "I think so. What the hell was that?"

"I have no idea. Can you move at all? Are you sure you're okay?"

Slowly, she lifted her head from his chest, and moved her neck and shoulders. "I'm good, I think. You?"

He did the same, bit by bit. When he was sure they were both in one piece, he slid from her body and rolled to one side on the sloped mattress.

"Well," he chuckled, running a hand through his dark hair. "I always said every time with you was pure magic."

She smacked him on the shoulder. "Funny. Not funny, Gareth."

"You know," he grinned at the look still on her face, "we're going to have to do this over and over again to find out what caused us to levitate. Scientific method."

She gritted her teeth, struggling to sit up on the broken slope. "I doubt scientists ever use the words levitate and science in the same sentence. This was magic. Sidhe magic. I just know it."

He cupped her chin, making her meet his eyes. "This wasn't Sidhe magic. It was you and me. Plain and simple. If Sidhe blood had anything to do with it, it's ours. Combined."

"Gareth, we've been *here* many, many times before, and we never had magical fallout. I know that was ten years ago, but—"

He put a finger over her lips. "Maybe this was pent-up foreplay, or a sexual logjam that finally burst. We can look it up in Magical Theory in the stacks, maybe give it a go again there."

She rolled her eyes, watching him waggle his eyebrows. "I've had plenty of sex since you disappeared into Faerie. Nothing close to this ever happened."

"That's because it wasn't with *me*," he replied. "We've both matured into our own. Our powers and abilities are fully fledged. Think about that."

She curled onto her side, facing him. "What are we going to tell Caitlan when she sees this mess?"

"I'm sure she already knows."

Lane rolled onto her back again. "Nice. I have to live with the woman."

"No, you don't." He pulled her toward him, his face serious. "You can live with me. The way it should have been from the start. We can live here, or if you want, I can try to take you with me to Faerie."

He kissed her softly, and the air shimmered gold again. This time the feel was light and playful, skimming their skin with tiny prickles that made her hair rise again.

"Well, wherever we are, one thing is for sure. We're going to need serious homeowners' insurance."

She grinned, kissing him back until the gold shimmer thickened and she could no longer think.

Chapter Nine

Gareth scanned the library's dusty stacks. "This place hasn't changed at all." He walked past the old archivist's desk piled with volumes. "I can still feel Grania's eyes watching us over the top of her horn-rimmed glasses." He winked.

"She wasn't the cheeriest of people, but she certainly knew her stuff." Lane dragged a finger over a shelf, leaving marks in the dust. She turned toward Gareth standing with his hands on the back of Grania's worn chair. "This place is in such confusion. I don't even know where to begin."

"Me neither, though Caitlan seemed to think we'd figure it out. Where is she anyway? I thought she said Caro left references for us somewhere." He lifted a book from the closest pile on the desk and flipped a few pages before dropping it back on the pile. The soft thud sent dust swirling and he sneezed.

"Dust comes with the territory, but God bless, anyway." Wiping her hands on her pants, Lane moved to the large study table at the center of the room.

"As promised, I guess." She tapped the small pile of old books and papers on the worn wood.

Lifting a handwritten note from the top of the low stack, she gave it a quick scan. "It's from Caro," she said, continuing. "She says the books she left for us reference the Circle of the Raven and our relationship to the Fae courts. She apologizes, saying it's not much, but considering we're Sidhe bastards, we shouldn't be surprised."

"Sidhe bastards." Gareth repeated the words matter-of-factly. "Funny how I wasn't made to feel that way in the Seelie Court. The Summer Queen welcomes Fae blood, no matter what."

"When it suits her agenda, I'm sure." Lane tucked the note into her back pocket. She didn't dare look at Gareth. Other than what she was taught and had read, she had no real knowledge of the Sidhe. Right now, she didn't care. Gareth was proof her bias rang true. It didn't suit their agenda to send word he survived, otherwise she and Caitlan would have known the moment he rose from the ashes.

A rare Fae Phoenix was a keeper. A real find, and everyone knew Sidhe royalty loved to *collect* the wonderous and unique.

"Let's divide and conquer this lot. You take one half, and I'll take the other." He joined her at the study table. "Caitlan can referee once she gets here."

Lane didn't reply. Instead, she grabbed one of the marked reference books and opened it to a marked page.

Since dropping his glamour, she'd barely had time to wrap her head around the fact of him. Maybe she didn't want to. Especially since the only thing she was interested in wrapping were her legs around his hips.

I have a few tricks up my sleeve I can't explain. Gareth's earlier words ran through her mind and they stopped her cold.

His eyes were gold. Sidhe gold.

No. Gareth is Gareth. He's the man I loved.

Still love.

Exactly. Why else is it too hard for you to contemplate? He said tricks, and Sidhe are master manipulators.

Stop it.

He's a Raven. Not a Sidhe.

Death by Sex doesn't mean actual death. It means losing oneself completely.

Isn't that a definition of love?

Stop being thick. You know I mean losing your identity. Becoming a slave. Like those vampires.

I'm not listening.

Fine. At least ask the questions that need asking. If not for yourself, then for Eve.

Shut up.

She winced. Her inner voice was right. She had to know, regardless of the answer. Gareth had come back from the dead and rocked her world. Not just between the sheets, but by resurrecting emotions she'd long buried. In her gut, she knew Gareth was connected to what happened with Eve. She sent up a silent prayer it wasn't her worst fears.

"You okay?" he asked. "You look like you're a million miles away."

Gareth touched her arm, and she nearly jumped out of her skin.

"Laney? What's going on?" He turned her to face him, slipping his hands to her waist.

She bit her lip. Her head screamed ask him and get it over with, but her body wanted his mouth and his hands. Was her attraction one of the tricks he couldn't explain? Some kind of low wattage Sidhe glamour, or was this real?

"Before we start on the books, you need to tell me why you showed up unannounced when you did. You said you were sent, but you really didn't go into detail."

It was clear on his face he saw she wasn't kidding. "I was told to keep things on the down low unless things went south."

"By south, you mean if Leith got what he came for." Lane eyed him closer.

He nodded. "But he didn't. You're still here."

The reference book was still in her hand, and she dropped it onto the others with an exhale. "Leith took Eve. That's close enough, and considering you said you were still all Raven, it should have been enough for you to tell me the truth."

"I've faced horrors and death. I've lived and survived in a place where many don't share the Seelie queen's beliefs. They view me as a half-breed abomination rather than a rarity. I've faced all that, but I wasn't brave enough to tell you what you needed to hear."

Lane's jaw tightened, but her eyes stayed riveted. "Eve's dead. You knew when you spotted me and decided to drop your glamour."

"No. I mean, it's a possibility, but I don't know for sure." Gareth exhaled, turning from her to pace by the darkened window. "The Seelie queen got wind of what happened in the Dark Court. Whispers are second nature to the Sidhe, and once in the air are hard to resist. But what Leith tried struck home. The Seelie queen met the Unseelie king in the lands between and struck a deal. Neither wants Leith's plan to succeed, as it threatens their shared tenets."

"What tenets? How can a single Raven make a difference to a millennia old race?"

Gareth stopped pacing and walked back to the table to ruffle through papers. "Damn. I didn't expect I'd find it here."

"What?"

He looked at her. "Records of what really happened with me. It's here—" he picked up the accounting again. "But it's incomplete. The same power the Unseelie tapped when they tried to harness my blood, my power, is the same magic Leith is trying to obtain. He knows the Unseelie failed with me, but he believes he'll be the one to unleash a power so great none can withstand. He's mad. But his genius is his determination. He won't stop until he's explored every possibility. And that includes you."

"My blood? Why? I'm nothing extraordinary. I'm a Raven, same as the rest. You were the unique one."

Gareth shrugged. "So, he thought. Now he's fixated on you. That's why I think it's more likely Eve is still alive. Killing her or letting her fall prey to his addicted vampires doesn't serve Leith's purpose. The answer has to be in these books somewhere. Raven lineage is a real thing, and there has to be a record of some sort hidden in this mess."

"If Leith is that sure of himself, then maybe he couldn't resist bragging about his plan. In his arrogance, maybe he shot off his mouth to add to

Eve's terror. Scare her into subservience for my sake."

He considered her words. "Definitely possible. It fits the profile information the Seelie Court provided before I hopped realms. This all happened moments ago for them, while for us it's been hours and hours."

She took the recorded pages from Gareth's hand and put them on the table. "Let's try scrying for Eve. This is our sanctuary and her essence is strong here. It might work."

"I guess." Gareth glanced at the shelves of old books and stacks of papers. "We can't use smoke or flame in here, but we can outside."

Lane shook his head. "Caitlan secured the grounds, but she's yet to perform the blood rite sealing the wards. She needed us for that," Lane replied low. "We took long—" she caught Gareth's eye and winked. "*Upstairs.*"

Turning on his heel, he stalked out the library door. Lane stared after him. "Damn."

He came back a moment later with one of the oval mirrors from the wall above the hall credenza. "Clear a space. Fire is best, but I'm not taking any chances with you. In this case a reflective surface will do us just fine."

Lane moved the books and papers Caro left for them to a chair.

"—and as for taking too long upstairs," Gareth continued, placing the mirror on the worn wood. "I plan on taking whatever time I can grab with you, as often as you allow. Wherever and whenever."

Stifling an inner squeal, she turned for Caro's teaching crystals on the desk. Grabbing a handful of amethysts and Herkimer diamonds, she carried the lot to the table.

"Since we can't burn incense, these will help. I don't know if you remember, but Herkimer are double terminated quartz. They're powerful, high vibration crystals that boost clairvoyant and clairaudient abilities. They're Eve's go to crystal and might help direct us to her."

"Every little bit helps."

Lane finished placing the crystals and then took her place beside Gareth. "Ready when you are."

"The summons is best in Latin," he said.

"And?"

He shrugged "Dead languages were never my strong suit."

"Confidence issues, Gareth? Are you afraid you'll conjure something I'll have to clean up?"

"No."

"Then just say you'd rather I do the honors."

His lips pushed into a *gotcha* smirk. "Well, your pronunciation was always better than mine. Besides, Eve doesn't even know me."

"Bock, bock," she teased. "How you can still charm me into doing things is beyond me."

In one fluid move, he skimmed her waist, turning her so close their breath mingled. "I don't want to charm you into anything. I want you willing and wet."

Her lips parted, waiting for the crush of his mouth, but footsteps outside the library door caught their attention.

"I was afraid you couldn't do this without adult supervision," Caitlan said as she entered. "Do I need to separate you two?"

Lane stepped back from Gareth with a cough. "Why would you think that?"

The look on the older witch's face said it all and Gareth grinned, unhooking his arm from Lane's waist.

"Caitlan's no fool, love. She's right. Hard as it is to concentrate, *you* need to focus."

"Me?" Lane sputtered.

"Okay, you two. Enough. The walls in this house are old and thin. Especially upstairs. I don't need or want any more details than I already have."

Lane groaned, but Gareth countered with a smirk. "I should be grateful Caitlan didn't turn you into a frog again."

"I'm a prince, babe."

Caitlan shut the banter down, holding her hands out for them to grasp. "Good choice on the crystals. Three times three times three. Let's begin."

Chapter Ten

"You sure this incantation has to be in Latin?" Lane ignored Gareth's smirk.

Caitlan looked at them both. "Who said a beckoning has to be in Latin?"

"Uhm, *you*," Lane countered with a snort.

Gareth nodded. "Every class. Every day."

She dismissed them outright with a ghost of a smirk. "Even if I did, you should be grateful I was such a stickler or you two would never have broken into the old stacks back in the day."

"You knew it was us?" Lane asked, surprised.

Caitlan shrugged. "Of course. What did you think?"

"All righty, then." Lane closed her eyes, holding tight to both their hands.

"Clear your mind and focus solely on Eve," Caitlan instructed. "Her essence. Her magic. They live in the fabric of this house. Grasp the common trace and will the images forth."

Gareth mumbled something and Lane cracked one eye open. "I thought you said you were crap at Latin?"

"I am, but one phrase I know by heart. *Viam sapientiae monstrabo tibi.* I will show you the way of wisdom."

Eyes closed, Caitlan flashed a soft smile. "It's nice to know someone was paying attention."

"Wow, Gareth." Lane snorted again." What's the Latin word for brown-noser?"

"Lane—"

"Sorry, Caitlan." She inhaled a breath before beginning the slow intonation. *"Obsecro per velamen, in quo mihi quaero. Visus revelare et dirige in via, semita ut nunc mihi.* Through the veil I beseech, show me the one in which I seek. Guide my sight and reveal the way, show me now, the path to take."

Three sets of eyes focused on the silvered glass. Lane repeated the Latin words, a mere whisper at first, but her call grew in tone and urgency as the mirror darkened to a glossy black.

The crystals glowed, ringing the scrying surface in crackling magic. "Look sharp," Caitlan warned. "Whatever shown us could vanish in an instant."

The black glass rippled like still water disturbed, as the first image cleared the darkness.

"Eve," Lane whispered.

Her friend was curled on a low palette surrounded by rushes on a stone floor. Fat, drippy candles burned in brass holders, and when she

looked closer, it was clear Eve suffered similar bites as Mason, though not fatal.

"Fucking Fae pig." Lane's voice cracked in anger. "He's let the vampires feed on her."

Caitlan studied the image as well. "The room looks medieval. Maybe he's got her holed up in the Cloisters over in Fort Tryon Park."

"It would serve Leith's purpose to keep this in our back yard," Gareth replied. "But truth is Eve could be anywhere. You forget the Sidhe can sift time. For all we know, the room looks medieval because it is medieval."

The glass rippled again. This time an image flashed of green hills cut by jagged, red cliffs. A dark sea battered the coastline, and Lane gasped at the accompanying sensation.

Desolation buffeted, but it disappeared as quickly as the image, leaving the mirror's surface cloudy and unreadable.

Black tendrils formed, swirling snake-like through the glassy murk. Lane shivered and gooseflesh spread across her skin. Her throat tightened as the dark harbingers rose.

"Gareth!" she croaked, squeezing his hand. "I can't stop them. What's hap...happen—" Her breath failed, and she pitched forward.

The crystals shattered, sending dirty gray fragments flying. Lane winced, blood trickling from where they bit into her flesh.

"Lane!" He twisted, trying to free his hand from Caitlan's grip, but she wouldn't let go. "I have to help her!"

"Gareth, no! If you break the circle, whatever holds Lane will take her completely. We are her only ground!"

Caitlan's words penetrated, and his jaw stiffened. Their blood mingled with Lane's and his eyes flashed liquid gold as the rivulets met. White hot power skittered over his skin, sizzling down his arm to his hand.

Hissing, Cait's muscles contracted against the surge, but she held tight. Iridescent energy spread, healing their wounds as it encompassed them whole, but pulled back when it swept toward Lane.

"He's stopping me from helping her!" With a snarl, Gareth ratcheted the surge, the intensity nearly bringing Caitlan to her knees.

"Save it, cowboy. Now is not the time for a power pissing match. Find another way!"

Lane whimpered, her veins straining in her throat as she tried to breathe.

"Show me what you see, Lane," Caitlan reassured. "Project the images like I taught you when you were a child. We can't help if we're fighting blind."

The encouragement was for Lane, but the arbitrating message was for Gareth. Don't poke the bear until cocked and ready.

"The bastard is using his power to—"

The supreme shot him a look, cutting off his words. "Brace yourself. I'm opening the channels!"

Caitlan withdrew the inner wards keeping the Fae magic at bay. They had to reach Leith before he reached them. It was the only way, if they wanted a shot at saving Lane from his grip.

Anger and dark lust flooded the open conduit to her mind, and the same cold, black tendrils clawed for her, but she was prepared.

Gareth gritted his teeth, fighting the attack as well, as Caitlan braced against the strike. Using all her skill, she isolated the intrusive sensations, redirecting to back-mind chambers.

The onslaught ebbed, and Gareth's relief was palpable. "Holy mousetrap, Batman, how did you do that?" He relaxed his grip, checking that Lane felt the temporary reprieve as well.

"Later. Right now, I need your power to help fight this bastard before he figures out my detour."

Gareth nodded, scowling. "I can taste his menace."

"Join the club. Weres got nothing on us when it comes to the tang of dark magic. When I give the word, send me everything you've got. Keep your grip tight on me and Lane, just in case."

His stony expression said it all. "Like iron. I want to see the bastard's face when we fry his Fae ass."

Caitlan's head yanked back and her body stiffened. She drew breath through her teeth, every muscle straining against an invisible force.

"Cait!"

Leith broke through her redirect, and a soft, cold laugh feathered through her mind. Painfully beautiful and unrelentingly erotic, he whispered in a language she didn't know, but somehow understood. Urgent and yearning, the murmurs buffeted her mind and teased her body, testing her reserve with hungry desire.

Supple and wet, the way you used to be. The way you wish to be. Want is swelling inside you, almost too much to bear. I feel it. You want my caress. My touch. You crave it. So easy to give in…to pleasure…to release. You know you have no choice.

Senses she thought long dead electrified her body, making her knees go weak. Invisible fingers stroked her nether flesh and the erotic punch left her breathless. She groaned, squeezing her eyes shut against the enticing sensations.

"He took Eve's power. She succumbed to him. Bastard seized her power when she…climaxed." Her words were clipped and tense. "Helpless and bound. I smell it through the mist. He's too strong."

Gareth gave her a vicious shake, bringing her back. "He's manipulating your senses, Caitlan. We're running out of time. We need to channel our combined power through to Lane. She knows what

to do. She reversed Leith's magic earlier tonight at the Red Veil."

From the dark glass, black tendrils spread higher, climbing toward Lane's throat and down to her sex.

Panic touched the young witch's eyes, begging for help. This was it. Gareth steeled himself, and then lifted his face and arms toward the ceiling, keeping their hands locked in his grip.

"Forgive me," he whispered.

The air hung heavy and still, like the calm before a storm. Soft, yellow light emanated from Gareth's skin, expanding until it encircled the three of them completely. It shimmered, warm and encompassing before spreading across the library.

Mad gusts tore at the room from nowhere, sending papers and books flying. The floorboards shook and glass panes splintered in the windows. The soft, buttery light surrounding them changed to an orange-gold, and Gareth's energy prickled across their flesh.

Power prickled with a thousand stings, narrowing tighter and tighter until it covered their bodies like a second skin.

"Caitlan! With me! Give it all to Lane! Now!"

Without hesitation, she lowered their linked hands, directing every ounce of power through to the younger witch.

Lane cried out at the unexpected flood, her flesh glowing bright and hot.

"Hold tight, love! We're fighting Fae fire with Fae fire. Phoenix style!"

Gareth's voice muffled in her ears. She knew he was there, but she could no longer feel his hands, or Caitlan's for that matter. She floated, her sight, and every other sense, blurred as she tried to focus on the dark glass.

Eve's image swirled in the murky depths for a moment, but then went black. Breathing hard, she tried to command the scrying glass, gathering the collective power swirling in her body.

"Show me what I seek!"

She had no sight, no voice, so the visions took her mind instead.

The mists cleared, only to show her friend was no longer alone in the stone room. A woman was with her, but who?

Ready power suffused her skin, but Lane froze as the woman turned. Her own face glanced back from the vision, and Lane nearly choked.

"Lane! Can you hear us?"

"Burn the bastard already!"

Gareth and Cait's voices barely penetrated as the image swirled and changed, but when she watched herself draw a short sword from its sheath beside the pallet bed, a silent scream ripped from her lips.

"Don't! Eve!" Shock and betrayal flashed in her friend's eyes as Lane watched the blade pierce Eve's chest. "It's not me! It's not true!"

Red anger bubbled hot, vibrating the amassed power waiting in Lane's chest. "No! You BASTARD!"

Collective energy exploded outward, its white heat incinerating the black tendrils holding her hostage. Lane collapsed in Gareth's arms as a loud hiss echoed in the chaos.

He held her tight, lowering her to the floor. "You had me worried there for a moment, kiddo. What the hell happened?"

Lane gripped his arms, her fingers buried in his biceps. "Leith had other plans for me."

Caitlan knelt beside her on the strewn papers. "We tried reaching you, honey, but your face...your eyes...they were blank and sightless. Where were you? What happened?"

She turned to meet Caitlan's worried eyes. "I was there. In the room with Eve. I killed her. Or I watched me do it."

"That's impossible. Even if you astral projected, you wouldn't be able to do anything but observe. You're not corporeal in that form."

Lane looked away. "I saw what I saw, Caitlan. I killed Eve."

"Eve isn't dead, Laney," Caitlan replied quickly. "I'd have felt it. When Ravens die, we all

feel the weight of their soul leaving. It's part of our shared lineage."

Lane met her gaze but didn't comment.

"Cait's right. Leith is a dark Sidhe. He's taken power from witches for longer than anyone knows for sure. Don't you think he could manipulate the power he took from Eve to make you think you killed her? Maybe in a moment of weakness and fear, Eve—"

"What?" Lane blurted. "Blamed me for getting her into this mess in the first place? That Leith used her blame and my guilt to make me think I killed her?"

Caitlan nodded sadly. "Yes."

"Even if my hand didn't plunge that blade into Eve's heart, she's dead because of me." Lane grunted a derisive snort.

"She's not dead, Lane," Caitlan tried again.

Gareth stood, reaching to help both women off the floor. "C'mon. We have work to do. You did not kill Eve, Laney. She gave us a hint."

"Hint?" Lane took his hand and let him pull her to her feet.

He nodded, helping Caitlan next. "She turned Leith's own deception back on him, using it to give us a hint on how to defeat him. Permanently."

"I think I'm starting to see what Gareth means," Caitlan surveyed the mess in the library. "Though,

the answer is going to be much harder to find in this clutter."

Bending to scoop up the pages on the floor around them, he straightened with a quick wink. "Not necessarily. Especially since we know what we're looking for now."

"Will one of you please explain to me what you're babbling about?"

He put the papers on the table next to the splintered scrying mirror, the spidery cracks distorting the normal reflection. "A sword."

Chapter Eleven

Caitlan crouched beside Lane, sorting through the scattered books on the floor by the study table. "If memory serves, there are only a handful of books that speak to the kind of weaponry resembling what you saw in your premonition."

"Well." Lane exhaled, tossing a book of random spells to the side. "They've got to be somewhere. The library's intact, just jumbled beyond recognition."

Caitlan snorted. "Tell that to Caro. Her categorization system is decimated."

"The sword in my premonition shined like polished silver. Maybe that's a clue and we should be looking for a book on metallic magical properties. The hilt has got to be a clue as well. It was even more ornate than your athame, Gareth."

He sorted books from the fallout on the opposite end of the room. "Silver is too soft a metal to be an effective weapon. The sword from your premonition was most likely carbon steel, which is iron ore based. I'd bet a testicle that's why *you* handled the sword in the vision and not Leith."

Caitlan nodded. "I agree with Gareth. We're looking for writings on a forged sword imbued with magical energy. Something a full-blooded Sidhe wouldn't dare risk touching." She paused, letting her gaze fall to Lane. "Try calling to it, honey. You're the one who saw the sword used. Visualize it. See it in the book that will tell us what we need."

"Anything's better than digging through this wreck." Resting her hands palm up on her knees, Lane rolled her shoulders and then closed her eyes. She muttered a soft spell awakening the part of her that knows, sees, and remembers everything.

"Silver moon, goddess wise, show me now within my right. Grant your blessing, three times three, show me now what I need. Crown chakra, knowledge bright, open now my third-eye's sight."

Power tingled her scalp, radiating through to her fingertips. They prickled as if already holding the book. She breathed slowly, in and out. Flashes formed, images flickering behind her lids as though the universe sorted the possibilities, discarding one after the other.

Caitlan stood, motioning to Gareth as a weak, winking glow peeked from beneath the bottom of one of stacks.

"Lane—" She kept her voice steady. "Whatever image is in your mind now, hold it. Expand it if you can, but don't let it go."

Caitlan moved toward the pile of books, bending to slowly remove each one until she stared at the glowing volume. Gold light shimmered from its spine and across its tatty cover. "Kids, I think we have lift off."

Lane exhaled, dropping her chin to her chest, murmuring a prayer of thanks to the universe. The image in her mind faded along with the tingle of power spiraling from her crown chakra, and she opened her eyes.

Unassuming in its design, the book had definitely seen better days. Its cloth cover was frayed along the edges, and time had rendered its title indiscernible.

Caitlan straightened with the book in her hand, turning to place it on the study table. She opened the cover with care, skimming the worn flyleaf before turning the first few delicate pages.

Lane and Gareth rounded the table to flank her on either side. "I wouldn't have given this a second glance," Lane murmured. "It looks too dogeared to be anything of significance." She reached to touch the delicate pages, but Caitlan smacked her hand.

"Gloves." The supreme nodded toward the desk. "In the top right drawer. The pages could be spelled or worse."

"*You* touched it," Lane grumbled, retrieving the gloves. "If the book was boobytrapped, you'd have

been zapped the moment you skimmed a hand over the cover."

Caitlan rolled her eyes. "Don't be a baby. Privilege comes with age and experience."

Lane handed gloves all around and then stood by as Caitlan turned threadbare page after page. Illustrations rivalling the hand-copied books of old winked from nearly translucent pages.

"This should be in a museum, not moldering at the bottom of a pile of reference books in a basement library," Lane replied, running a gloved finger over the vivid gold and red ornamental lettering.

The illustrations depicted weapons of all shapes and sizes. From easy to conceal dirks to heavy claymores and thrusting longswords, along with techniques for block, swing, parry and thrust.

"So, the book the universe wanted us to find the medieval version of *Swordplay for Dummies*." Lane shifted the book for a closer look. "Okay, fates. What now?"

She skimmed the descriptions before gently turning the next few pages. "This is nothing but general descriptions of when and how to use the weapons. Plus, none of them fit what I saw exactly. The sword I wielded had Fae sigils in gold on the hilt, and other sigils I couldn't recognize engraved on the flat of the blade. On top of everything, we still don't know why Leith wants me in particular.

I was hoping Caro's research could shed some light on that, but I guess not."

Caitlan walked toward the only shelf in the library with books still intact. They were so because they were encased in leather and glass. "Lane, how much do you remember from when you first came to the motherhouse?" Taking a key from a chain hidden in her cleavage, she unlocked the small bolt at the bottom of the case.

"Not much. I remember you and Grania. Gareth came later, but other than that—" Lane shrugged.

Caitlan lifted the glass lid to the case. "I'm not surprised."

"Does this have something to do with Leith and why he's wreaking havoc?" Gareth asked, his interest piqued as well.

"In a nutshell, yes." Caitlan took the books from inside the case, one by one, placing them on a chair. "You were brought here by your mother. Her name was Aislinn."

Lane's mouth opened but she snapped it closed at the look on Caitlan's face.

"She was a Raven, like you. Beautiful. Ethereal. Her one flaw was not knowing her own worth. She needed physical validation, and eventually it went way beyond sexual satisfaction. She fell prey to a Sidhe, and succumbing, eventually became enslaved." Her eyes were sad. "You know the type.

Death by sex. Except your mother didn't die. She became pregnant.

"It was the life stirring within her, your life, that brought her to her senses. Aislinn escaped your father, never telling him of your existence. She did her best to raise you alone, but as you got older, she knew it was only a matter of time before he sensed you. Before puberty hit, and you came into your power.

"Aislinn showed up on our doorstep with you in tow. You weren't more than six or seven years old. Together we bound your Sidhe side, only allowing your witchy powers to manifest. It's the same with Gareth."

At Lane's sharp intake, Caitlan whirled on her heel.

"Relax, Gareth is *not* your brother. But he is a halfling, same as you. He has enough Sidhe blood to be claimed. Just as you do. Your mother didn't want that."

"So, she made the choice for me? From what you describe, I'm her polar opposite. I don't need validation from anyone but myself, let alone physical validation from sex. Hell, I frequented the backrooms at the Red Veil to get my freak on because it's what I wanted, not because I needed to feel good about myself."

Caitlan stood beside the empty case. "Not because you were trying to escape something?"

Her eyes slipped to Gareth. "Memories of what might have been, perhaps?"

Lane didn't answer, and Caitlan took that as a cue to continue. "Your mother had good reason to choose for you. Gareth is male. And a rare Phoenix. It's why the Seelie queen accepted him into her court. You're female, so you'd have no choice but to be a concubine or a despised servant, especially since your bloodline hailed from the Unseelie court. Aislinn wanted you to have a choice in life, Lane. As a Raven, you could one day be a supreme, or more."

Gareth slipped an arm around Lane's slumped shoulders, supporting her under the weight of Caitlan's revelations. "Are you telling us Leith is Lane's father?"

"Yes." She nodded. "Earlier, I told you we needed a blood rite. I let you believe it was to protect the motherhouse and our coven, and I'm sorry for the lie of omission. The blood rite we need is to unbind Lane's Sidhe powers so the two of you can defeat Leith together. The blood rite will coalesce your powers and unlock your Fae side, but the only way to ensure you don't fall prey to what your father wants, you'll need to be claimed."

At that, Lane's shoulders stiffened, and her eyes jerked to Caitlan. "Claimed? By whom? How?"

"By another Sidhe."

Gareth spared a tentative glance for Lane. "Full-blooded?

"No." Caitlan met Gareth's eyes. "By you. You've been claimed by the Seelie Court, so by default you may claim a mate. Considering you were sent by your queen, I doubt she'll have much to say against the proposal. If we do the ritual correctly, Leith won't be able to resist trying to disrupt things."

Gareth looked at Lane. "You look like you're going to vomit. Bad idea?"

"No, it's what I've always wanted, it's just—" she licked her lips. "Not like this. Like we have no other choice."

He squeezed her shoulder, pressing a kiss to her hair. "Shotgun wedding, Fae style. Besides, you're the one who said you wanted to be bait."

Her head jerked around, and she met his eyes. "The vampires. We've completely left them out of the equation. They're going to want their pound of flesh, not to mention the Weres. Leith manipulated the three vamps he used to get to me, putting a very important truce at stake. Pardon the pun."

"If you're suggesting what I think you're suggesting, then I'm not sure I'm okay with it, Lane. The motherhouse has never hosted vampire guests, or shifters for that matter. I'm not so sure they'd be happy with the idea either."

"Then we'll have to rethink the plan of attack," Gareth interjected. "We still have to find the right weapon in this book and see what it has to say. In the meantime, we should contact the vampire council and the Alpha of the Brethren."

"Gareth's right. You've had enough for one twenty-four-hour period. I'll make the necessary calls. Leith is a consummate chess player, and this is a game for him. The board is ours for now. He can't make a move until we do, so get some rest. We can put together what we need for the ritual come morning. The house and grounds are completely warded, so sleep well." Caitlan winked. "I'll leave you two to it, then."

Gareth turned with Lane for the door, but Caitlan stopped them. "Just one more thing."

She waved a hand inside the empty glass and leather case, muttering a spell under her breath. A letter appeared, and she took it and the sword book and handed them both to Lane.

"It's from Aislinn. She left it for you to open when the time came for your powers to be woke. Read it and then look through the book. I have a feeling you'll find the all the answers you need."

Chapter Twelve

"Why don't you take a hot shower? It'll help." Gareth's fingers wrapped around her shoulders with a light squeeze. "Your head has to be spinning with what Caitlan revealed."

Lane inhaled, letting her head drop so his fingers kneaded more of the tension from her neck. "That's putting it lightly. Finding out my biological father is a Sidhe psychopath doesn't do much for my self-esteem. Especially since I've been the black sheep around here forever."

"Bending the rules doesn't make you a black sheep. You've never hurt anyone intentionally, and your heart was always in the right place."

"I suppose." She paused, cocking her head to glance at him from the side. "How come you didn't seem quite as stunned when Caitlan let my parentage out of the proverbial bag?"

He slid an arm forward, holding her against his chest. "Because I already knew."

His breath tickled the back of her ear, and she turned in his embrace to look at him eye to eye. "You knew?"

He nodded, cupping her cheek. "When word of Leith's attempt to bring about a coup reached the Summer Kingdom, the Seelie Court was a buzz. To be honest, I didn't pay much attention until I heard one name mentioned."

"Mine."

"Yes. At that point, I used every connection I had to find out whatever I could. The queen was the one who finally told me. Apparently, she knew about you from the beginning, including where you were all this time." He hesitated, letting go of her cheek. "She was the one who helped Aislinn get away from Leith. I guess she felt sorry for her in some small way, which is saying a lot because the Fae aren't exactly compassion incarnate. Just the opposite."

She pulled out of Gareth's grip. "Great. This just gets better and better."

"Laney, don't." He let her slip past but held onto her hand. "Which do you think holds more sway over who we become? Nature or nurture? You're still the same amazing woman you were twenty-four hours ago, right? Who cares if you've got Sidhe blood? I don't, and I'm in the same halfling boat as you.

"I told you before all this came to light. Before Caitlan even mentioned the possibility of us claiming each other. I want you. I've always wanted you. It's what should have been from the

beginning and can be now." He paused, pulling her closer again. "Are you trying to tell me you don't want this? Don't want to be with me?"

His eyes searched hers, and the heat coming from his body and his gaze seared her soul and made her flesh ache for his touch.

"Uhm, I think I'm going to take that shower."

"Good. It'll help you relax. Maybe even help you sleep."

Lane shook her head. "A shower isn't going to do it for me, Gareth. I need something hard to work out these knots." She reached up and undid one tie at the top of her blouse, letting the soft fabric slip past one shoulder. "Something really hard."

She undid the second tie, letting her shirt slip to her waist in a silken fall. "How did you put it earlier? Hard enough to cut diamonds?" Reaching for the front of his pants, she hooked her fingers into his waistband. "Any ideas?"

"Plenty." Gareth slid his hands to her waist, letting his lips hover just above her mouth. "First off, you have too many clothes on," he tsked. "What are we going to do about that?" He reached for her blouse and tugged it over her head, letting the fabric fall to the floor. Unhooking her bra, he dipped his head to her jutting nipples, nipping them each through the lace until she moaned, arching her back.

He walked her backwards into the bathroom, leaving her bra on the floor with her blouse. There was

enough ambient light from Lane's bedroom to set everything in warm, luscious shadow. His mouth crushed hers, devouring her lips and her tongue as he reached behind her back to turn on the spray. Steam rose almost immediately, bathing her exposed flesh in a gorgeous sheen.

Dragging his fingers over her full breasts, he circled her nipples with the wet condensation. "I want more than just your tits wet and on display, Laney. I want your pussy dripping. Spread wide for me to take and taste. There's something primal about fucking in water. Primitive. Ravaging. And I want it all. I want you wild with desire, your pussy so wet it slicks your thighs and drips over my chin and then later my balls."

Lane gasped and her nipples and clit throbbed from just his words. A single touch and she'd come like a rocket. Gareth's lips pushed into a smirk. "Strip, Lane. Leave on nothing but your panties."

She did as he asked, and he kissed her again but stepped back instead of escalating to the next level. Her mouth dropped to complain but stopped when she saw he went to the sideboard across from her bed.

"Lots of interesting things you've got hidden in the cupboard, little girl," he teased, resting a half-empty bottle of wine and a small, drawstring bag on the shower's tile floor. "Plus, I never let a good merlot go to waste."

He stepped back, untying the drawstring to his pants before slipping them past his hips. He did so slowly, teasing Lane completely as his fingers pushed the soft cotton past the sexy vee and tease of dark hair toward the hard length waiting below.

"You're killing me, Smalls." She flashed a smirk, quoting their movie as he did earlier.

His cock sprang free of the restrictive waistband, the hard bar thick and corded.

Lane licked her lips. *Smalls* was definitely not a word to describe Gareth. It never was.

His grin faded to an urgent slash and he scooped her into his arms and stepped over the edge and into the spacious open shower.

The water beaded on her skin, cascading in rivulets drenching her hair. He leaned down, taking one nipple between his teeth. He sucked the stiffening peak between his lips, letting one hand dip between her thighs.

Stroking her wet slit, he slipped two fingers into her cleft and curled them deep. He leaned in, taking her mouth as he circled her inner spot. "I want you on your knees, Lane. Your ass in the air. You're mine. Every inch of you."

He broke their kiss and pulled back his hand, licking each one before kissing her again. "The taste of you makes my cock want to burst. For years, I imagined how you smelled, your taste. Alone I worked my length to just your memory and every sense I could

conjure. Now I have you here, in the flesh, and I want every inch of you."

Her heart pounded in her chest, but a secret smile stole across her lips as she kissed Gareth's neck, feathering tiny bites and kisses down his chest as she sank to her knees in front of him.

"Not so fast, love." He stopped her, pulling her to her feet again. "Me first."

His voice was commanding. Earlier it was just urgent, but now it was clear the sexy boy she loved, lusted for, and lost had grown into a man's man, with scars inside and out to match. Power rippled beneath her fingers as she explored his muscled torso and chest. She got to her feet, and the heat of his gaze locked her breath in her throat, nearly scorching her flesh. His eyes took in her full length, lingering at the way the spray glistened on her body, wet and bidding.

With one fluid motion, he swept her up again, sitting her on the marble bench at the back of the shower stall. He knelt and pushed her thighs apart. Dipping his face to her slick folds, he licked her slit to her hard nub. "You take my breath away, Lane. I could bury myself in you forever and never have enough."

She sucked in a breath, his words and the rough feel of his beard on her tender flesh pushing her higher toward climax. Closing her eyes, she let her head drop back as he slid his thumb between her folds. "So fucking wet," he whispered, letting his fingers slide further to circle her clit. "But we can do better."

He took the wine bottle from the floor of the shower and pull the cork with his teeth, spitting it to the floor. Pouring the wine over her breasts, it trickled to her pussy in purple rivulets.

Gareth sucked her tits, licking and nibbling his way to her slippery, wine-soaked mound. "Sweet musk and sweet wine. You intoxicate me, Lane. In all ways."

She arched back, moaning as his fingers and mouth drove her pussy. Gareth slid his free hand over her belly to cup her breast, and she dug her fingers into her dark hair, grinding herself farther into his mouth. She came hard as he sucked her clit deep, gasping as spasms shook.

He pulled back, wiping his mouth on the back of his hand with a satisfied grin. "So damn good, but now it's my turn." Pushing her knees wide, he got to his feet and wrapped his hand around his corded shaft.

Stepping between her thighs, he pressed the tip of his cock to her lips and Lane took his full length, no waiting. She wrapped her hands around his ass, working him with the flat of her tongue and her throat. Milking his corded length, she slid him even deeper before releasing him inch by inch until the ridged edge of his head bulged between her lips ready to blow.

A muffled gasp left Gareth's throat. "Woman, unless you want to swallow everything I give, you'd better spread yourself now!"

He didn't wait for an answer. He pulled his cock free and yanked her to her feet, crushing his mouth to

hers, fierce and exacting. The salty taste of his essence was on her lips and it mixed with her nuance still on his tongue.

Breaking their kiss, he turned her so her back molded against his chest. "I want you on your knees, Lane. Your ass grinding my cock."

Nipping the back of her neck, he urged her to the tile. With a single thrust, he drove his member between her folds, his hips pumping hard and fast.

Gareth filled every inch of her core. Lane's breath locked in her throat as she came again, her hips meeting his thrust for thrust. Pleasure flooded her body as it quaked and squeezed.

He reached for the drawstring bag on the floor. "Feel like a walk on the wild side, little witch?" He drew a large dildo from inside the bag, curved with tiny nubs along the synthetic skin shaft. "You had quite a selection, but I thought this one looked like the most fun."

He pulled his cock back, taking a moment to spread her slick wetness back toward her tight hole.

Teasing her, he worked her ass with his thumb as he worked her pussy with the tip of the dildo. She moaned at the invasive feel as his fingers stretched her tight ring, readying her for his thick dick. He drew the fleshy plastic back from her sex and then helped her to all fours on the bench. Pressing the tip of his cock to her hole, he slid inside, inch by straining inch. She took

him, sucking sharp breaths as her body hovered between pleasure and pain.

"So fucking tight," he whispered behind her ear as he teased her clit before slipping the dildo between her folds again.

With a deep thrust, he buried his length in her tight sheath, riding her ring as he worked her pussy. She moaned at the combined feel of his cock and the sexy toy, both filling beyond measure.

Every muscle tensed, suspended, until pleasure tore through her, radiating hot and fierce. Waves spread through her lower belly and down her thighs, penetrating her core as Gareth impaled her body over and over.

The tiled shower shimmered gold and white as power sizzled in and around them. It spiraled, sizzling on their skin. Gareth held tight. Every muscle coiled as her climax rocked through him. He let go with a cry, hot jets pulsing deep within her.

With a gasp, he let the dildo slide free. It splashed to the shower floor as he tightened one arm around Lane's waist. Cupping her pussy with the other, they rode the final waves together until they both slumped forward in the warm spray.

The two lay panting, their bodies entwined and sweaty as water cascaded around them. Gareth released her waist, slowly slipping his member from her tight ring. He reached for the bodywash on the

shelf and lathered his hands, sliding the whip cream bubbles over Lane's breasts and between her legs.

She did the same, washing him as well. His lips found hers, and he kissed her soft and warm. "I love you, Lane Alden. I always have and I always will, and I am never letting you go."

Tucking herself beneath his arm, she wrapped soapy hands around his back, holding him tight. "Good, or I'll make Caitlan turn you into a frog for good."

He smiled against her hair, kissing the wet mass. "You'd kiss me into a prince again. I know you. You could never resist having the last word."

Lane slid her slippery hands around to his still thick member. "That's not the only last I couldn't resist."

Kissing her again, Gareth lifted her with a quick spin, pressing her back to the warm tile wall and his cock to her waiting pussy. He fucked her slow and languorous, teasing her with every stroke until neither could take anymore. They climaxed again, power surging between them, sending glittering light circling like constellations as they came.

He buried his head in her neck, a smile stretching across her wet skin. "I don't think we're going to need Caitlan's blood rite to waken your Sidhe side."

She laughed. "Why? You afraid of a little blood?"

"No. But it might be an overstatement at this point. Your skin is glowing gold, love. I think we accomplished the deed all by ourselves."

Lifting her arm, Lane grinned, watching her skin shimmer and sparkle. "Oh man, Caitlan's going to be so mad."

He laughed. "I don't think she'll care. She might even make us go through the motions just to be sure it's not a one off."

Cupping his wet face, she kissed him again, biting his bottom lip. "I am not a one off. You are not a one off. *We* are not a one off. Got it?"

"Yes, ma'am. Now let's get out of this water. It's going cold and my bits are starting to shrivel…and that's an *off* neither of us want."

Chapter Thirteen

*L*ane lay on her pillow, propped against the headboard. Gareth snored gently beside her, but she couldn't sleep. Too much had happened too quickly for rest to come.

She flipped through the channels on the television, but nothing interested her. Too preoccupied to give late night programming more than a cursory glance, her eyes swept to the desk across the bedroom, and the book and the letter sitting on top of Gareth's pile of clothes.

With a tentative breath, she swung her legs over the side of the bed and padded over to carry them back to the bed with her.

The letter had her name scrawled in big, looping script across the front, with a small heart drawn into the cursive letter E at the end of her name. She ran her fingers over the ink, wondering what her mother's thoughts were at the time. From what Caitlan said, she already knew her fears.

The generous handwriting and the drawn heart reminded her of commercials where moms hid tiny love notes inside their children's lunchboxes. Her

heart squeezed at how she never knew what it felt like to have that kind of unconditional love. To have a mom.

Staring at the cursive heart, she knew now she had that all along, albeit from afar. Her throat tightened at the realization, and she didn't know whether to laugh, cry, or kill something. She'd been robbed, and it was Leith who was responsible.

Caitlan didn't say much more after her initial revelation. In fact, she didn't explain what happened to Aislinn after she and Caitlan bound her Sidhe powers. Maybe it was too painful. Or perhaps Caitlan didn't know. Maybe she thought the weight of the disclosure was enough for one night.

Either way, Leith was responsible no matter what happened. If Aislinn hadn't felt trapped and threatened, she'd never have been compelled to run.

"Like ripping off a Band-Aid," she murmured under her breath, and tore the envelope open across the top.

She pulled the thin cream-colored sheet from the inside and unfolded it to the same looping script.

My darling daughter,

If Caitlan revealed this letter, then your father has found you and I failed. Your safety and happiness are my

only concerns, even if it means exchanging my life for yours.

You are my heart, my life and my hope, and the only reason I have to hold tether to this world. The choices I have made have been foolish and vain. I'm paying a heavy price for my mistakes by leaving you with the Ravens. It is the only way I know to guarantee your safety. By sacrificing my own weakness, I pray it gives you the courage and strength you'll need to make your life a success. My wish for you, my baby girl, is to find your true self and cherish who you are, and that in doing so you find love deserving of you. Never forget who you are, even when tempted. Know from this moment you were cherished above my own life. Loved and wanted.

Your father wasn't always a cruel being, but his Fae nature was corrupted and eventually his machinations and manipulations consumed him. He thought to make me a slave, and if he had an inkling of your existence, he would do the same with you. Me to do his bidding, and you to use as a pawn where he saw fit. I couldn't allow that. I sealed my own fate when I succumbed to him, but you, my darling, are an innocent. Fae blood may course through your veins, but you are a Raven, and that will give you the strength you need to overcome whatever poison Leith brings to your doorstep.

It is why I made the decision to bind your Sidhe side. Caitlan wasn't happy about the choice, but in the end, she knew it was the only way to protect you. Binding your Sidhe powers will buy you the time to develop as a

Raven, and to find and cherish your inner strength and self-worth.

My only regret is I won't be with you to share in your accomplishments, to hug away your fears and worries, and to give you the mother's love you so deserve. I've made the choice to go back to Faerie. It's the second half of the sacrifice necessary to keep you safe. In my gut I know I'm not long for either plane, but if the fates smile on us and we meet again, I hope you can find it in your heart to forgive me.

Your loving mother,

Aislinn.

An ache washed through her along with grief so deep, the only thing large enough to fill the hole was anger. Lane folded the letter, slipping it into the envelope. Dropping it on the nightstand, she stared impotent at the ceiling.

"Fuck this," she muttered, and got up from the bed.

Pulling on a pair of leggings, she then pulled a sweatshirt over her head and shoved her feet into her sneakers. She took the book of swords from the bed and left the bedroom, careful not to wake Gareth.

Her mind swirled. Her mother gave her up to protect her because she wasn't strong enough to fight. Wasn't strong enough or maybe she simply didn't know how. That was about to change.

Lane headed back to the library. She knew the why, now she needed to know the how. The puzzle in her head was almost complete. The means to fight the bastard that robbed her mother of her will, and then robbed *her* of her mother, had been revealed in her vision. All that was left was to find the weapon and teach daddy dearest a lesson he'd never forget.

Light peeked from the bottom of the library door, and she paused to listen. There was no sound or movement and she sent her senses out to make sure.

Nothing.

Caitlan must have left a light on, knowing she'd read the letter and not be able to sleep.

She slipped quietly through the door and settled in a chair at the study table. Years ago, she'd sit in this very spot with friends, laughing in whispers at old Grania chewing on her dentures. Later, she sat with Gareth, both pretending to study while their hands explored hidden delights under the table.

Opening the book again, she skimmed every page. The ornate lettering was hard to read at first, but she focused on her quarry, hoping her new Sidhe senses would give her a little help.

She had no idea how to channel that power or even control it a little. The thought was disconcerting at the least and downright terrifying

at most. She joked about the dark side, but being a Dark Fae halfling, could she fall prey to the same temptations that corrupted her father? Was it so easy? Part of her nature? Or was Gareth correct in that she had the best of both now, being raised as a Raven?

Focusing her senses, she pulled from the well of power deep within and pictured the sword and all its parts. The sigils on the pommel and the Fae wording on the blade.

She flipped to the center of the book and the most colorful spread in the volume. The painted illustration showed a hollow, with a sword depicted piercing what looked to be an ancient Faerie mound. The blade was the right length and breadth, but everything else was wrong.

Closing her eyes, she focused on the gold light that emanated from her skin in the shower. Let it bathe her mind, color everything with its sheen.

In that moment, the individual pieces of the image broke apart, reforming to show a labyrinth of trees and flowering bushes leading to latticed grotto. There was no mound in sight, but a rose-covered building similar to a gazebo sat at the end of the path.

She opened her eyes, and what she saw in her mind was depicted on the page, and inside the glass house was the sword.

"That looks very much like the Peggy Rockefeller Rose Garden at the New York Botanical Gardens. With one exception. It's completely enclosed and there are no doors."

She jumped, puffing out a startled breath as she saw Gareth peering over her shoulder. "Don't do that! Jeez."

"Sorry. I couldn't resist." He chuckled, pressing a kiss to her temple. "Are you okay? I woke up and you were gone."

She nodded. "I opened the letter."

"I saw."

Cocking her head, she eyed him from over her shoulder. "Did you read it? It's okay if you did, I mean I left it there in the open."

"No. Whatever it says is between you and your mom. You can tell me about it when you're ready."

His hand was on her shoulder and she pressed her cheek to it. "God, I love you."

One finger caressed the curve of her face. "Back atcha, love."

Lane breathed in his warm scent and then straightened. Refocusing, she tapped the book. "You said this looks familiar?"

Gareth inched the edge of the cover around to see better. "Yes. Like I said, the Rose Garden. But I don't remember this being in the book last night. Is it a different volume?"

"Nope. I zinged it with some newfound power and the page sort of rearranged itself. Must have been a spell that needed a halfling to work."

Gareth turned the book fully. "This is telling us one of three things. The sword is hidden here, or this is a Faerie mound or portal of some kind needed to find the sword, or it's both."

"Do you have your cell phone?" she asked.

Raising an eyebrow, he pulled his cell from his back pocket. "This isn't *Who Wants to be a Millionaire*, you can't phone a friend, Lane."

With a smirk, she snatched the iPhone from his hand. "You're cute, you know that?"

Snapping a picture of the image, she turned the camera horizontal to check. "Shit."

"I tried to tell you. Real magic can't be captured, even with today's digital knowhow." Gareth took the book from the table and tucked a placeholder into the crease marking the page. "The only technologies to even come close are Krilian Aura Photography, and the Ovilus for synthesizing EMF waves to speech."

"You've got to be kidding. We're the real deal, Gareth, yet you're talking cold spots and microwave interference. This isn't ghost hunting."

He chuckled. "Sounds like I hit a major sore spot. Of course, we're the real deal, but paranormal investigators aren't wrong. Things that go bump in the night are very much a part of

our world." He slipped his arms around her waist from behind. "Although, I prefer our way of going bump in the night to theirs any day. Much more satisfying."

"Keep your head in the game, horn ball. We can play bump uglies again later. Right now, I want to head to the Botanical Gardens and check out this Rockefeller Rose Garden. According to Google, it doesn't open for a couple of hours yet, so until then we should research whatever we'll need to take with us in case it turns out to be a portal. The last thing I want is to get caught in a supernatural vortex between Faerie and here, and not have the sword."

"Vortex? I'm guessing you watch a lot of *Dr. Who*." He kissed the top of her head and reached for his phone on the table in front of her to double check the website.

She smirked, leaning back into his chest. "Hey, no hating on the good doctor. She's terrific."

"She?" he questioned.

"Yup. You don't have a problem with that, right?"

He chuckled behind her ear. "No, ma'am." Pausing, he crouched over her shoulder to better look at the website on his cellphone. "You do realize the Botanical Gardens closes at six pm."

"And?"

"We'll need to break in after dark if we expect to get anything done."

She nodded. "This time of year, it stays light until about seven thirty pm or so. If Caitlan called the Red Veil to fill the vampires in on what happened, they could help us big time once it gets dark. Until then, you and I can do a little recon to help set the stage."

In that moment, he spun her around and she immediately went up on tip toe to peck his lips. "So, big boy. Fancy a stroll through the park with me? Who knows, maybe you'll get lucky with a little afternoon delight."

Gareth smiled. "It's a date, but right now I think we need a little sleep. Yawning during a seduction is not exactly a turn on, so shut eye first. Afternoon delight with a little recon, later.

"Fine. I hope you know I expect spooning, right?"

He swung his arm around her shoulders and steered Lane toward the doors and their waiting bed upstairs. "If it means you in my arms...deal."

Chapter Fourteen

"What's all this?" Lane asked as she climbed into the cab.

Gareth moved the wicker basket to the opposite side of the back passenger seat, and then held out a hand to help her settle.

"I scavenged the larder for a picnic lunch. A romantic gesture, even if I say so myself." He clicked his cheek. "With the other initiates sequestered to safe houses around the city, the food just sat in the fridge. I thought why not pack it up and take it with us to the park?"

She closed the cab door. "Because this is a scouting assignment, not a date."

"Ha. Says the woman whose first thought when we planned this outing was public lewdness and a possible misdemeanor charge."

"Wow, Golden Boy. Way to suck the romance right out of an afternoon delight."

He swept her blonde hair behind her ear, tracing the curve of her jaw. "Sorry, love, but you can't call me that anymore."

"Golden Boy?"

He nodded. "You've conveniently forgotten that magical shimmer that rose to a gorgeous flush once you reached—"

"Ssh! Gareth!"

The cab driver glanced at them from the rearview wearing an amused smirk. "Where to, Mac?"

"New York Botanical Gardens, please," Gareth answered the man, trying not to chuckle.

The cab pulled into the street and began crosstown maneuvers to get to the West Side Highway northbound toward the Bronx.

"Great. Now the whole city knows I flush pink and gold in the heat of the moment." Lane hid her face in her hands.

Smirking, Gareth closed the small plexiglass divider between the front and the back of the cab. "*Thar* she glows, like a true Sidhe halfling."

"Funny. You make a Moby Dick analogy and I'm supposed think that's cute."

"It is cute, and so are you. Look on the bright side. If we don't get to the Bronx soon, the whole city will know you make my Moby Dick swell to bursting just by sitting beside me. Takes an awful lot of sexy to do that."

Gareth pressed a kiss to her temple, and she inhaled his clean, freshly showered scent, very much aware of his muscled thigh against her leg.

"I guess a picnic isn't such a bad idea. I mean, who am I to turn down an alfresco meal? We need to eat anyway, right?"

With a hand on her thigh, he let his fingers steal closer to the juncture between her thighs. "We definitely need to eat."

She turned to meet his blue eyes but didn't stand a chance as his lips claimed hers. He took her mouth with skill and command, but his kiss tasted as though he was holding something back. As if savoring a secret.

When he broke their kiss, she sat back with an uneven breath. "Damn, Gareth. Forget the Bronx. We might have to ward the cab and every place in between."

With a grin, he took her hand, pressing a kiss to her knuckles. "Not every place, Goldilocks. We'll find a spot that's just right. Not too hard. Not too soft."

She winced.

"That bad?"

"Awful."

He shook his head, but his teasing grin stayed widened. "C'mon. Admit it. That was cute. The whole fairy tale thing? Considering we're Faeries?"

"I'll give you five out of ten. With extra points for trying."

"Extra points?" He reached over, pulling her onto his lap. "How about I show you just how much extra I can be."

***

"Oh, man. You have got to be kidding me." Lane threw up a hand, as Gareth came up behind carrying two ice cream cones.

"What?" he asked, licking the edge of one before handing the other to Lane.

"That." She pointed to the Peggy Rockefeller Rose Garden, and the parade barricades and construction mesh blocking public access.

"Pardon our Appearance." She read the sign on the gates featuring a sepia-tone image of the Rose Garden from 1916.

With a curse, she leaned against the curved bluestone wall from the overlook above the Rose Garden. "Well, at least we know what we're up against."

"That green blob must be the gazebo." Gareth pointed with his ice cream toward the dull green tarpaulined dome peeking above the construction.

"The website didn't mention renovations. What do we do now?" Lane asked, squinting to better survey the area.

This area of the Botanical Gardens wasn't crowded, and now they knew why. Everywhere else, children walked in clusters as their teachers led class trips through the different exhibits. Others

meandered the paved paths, but no one bothered with the cordoned off Rose Garden. There wasn't much to see. At least not for another month when the exhibit was set to reopen.

"June." Lane shook her head at the date posted on the sign. "We can't wait that long. Eve is still alive, at least that much we know. Caitlan and I scried for her again before you and I took off. We couldn't pinpoint her location, but we sensed her essence enough to satisfy she's still breathing."

Gareth took her hand. "C'mon." He tugged her away from the bluestone wall and steered her down the steps. "We need to take a closer look. We might be able to sneak in around the back. If the crew working this renovation is like other state-run projects, chances are they're milking the governmental cow. Wasted time and resources is the name of the game when taxpayers foot the bill, so we might have a shot."

They circled the path, but voices and machinery were muffled through the solid fencing, and Gareth swore. "The one time I need systematized laziness on my side, and everyone suddenly develops a work ethic."

"Did you honestly expect this to be easy? This isn't Hollywood meets the Fae version of *National Treasure*. We are going to have to break a few rules to get that sword and defeat Leith."

She stood with her hand half-raked through her hair. "You're not the only one who hoped we could do this now and be done, but it looks as if Caitlan was right. We need to come back tonight, and we're going to need the vampires for cover."

Walking twenty or so paces across the main grass, he left the paved path behind and stood for a moment listening, before jogging back.

"There's heavy traffic in that direction, so we can assume the highway is that way." He pointed toward the area behind them.

She nodded. "The Bronx River Parkway. Why?"

"Okay, then." He circled back toward the path again but this time he went in the opposite direction. "So, if the parkway is to the east, then the river running through the Gardens runs parallel."

"The Bronx River. It has the same name because, yes, it runs parallel to the highway, but what has one got to with the other, and why does it matter? We need a plan, not a topography lesson."

He jogged back, taking both her hands in his. "That's what I'm driving at. If we can't get into that gazebo in a straightforward manner, then we need to do so with stealth. This is a state park. Which means it has pretty tight security. The best way for us to sneak in is via the water. Flowing water carries magic. The Bronx River is all we've got. It's polluted, but it will still amplify vampiric glamour

and whatever wards we conjure enough to do the trick."

Gareth's enthusiasm exuded confidence and strength, and she pictured him striding in the Faerie Courts like a magical medieval knight. The image was such a turn on, it left butterflies winging through her stomach.

"Uhm, speaking of warding large ribbons of ground and water." She rubbed her thumbs in sexy circles over his hands. "Aren't you hungry?"

She raised an eyebrow and his lips pushed to the side in a sexy crooked half-smile. "After all that foreplay in the cab? I'm surprised you even have to ask."

Without another word, he tossed her over his shoulder and jogged with her toward a cluster of secluded trees toward the back of the property.

"Gareth! Put me down!"

He let her down at the base of a large oak. "Pretty, huh?" Not waiting for her to reply, he turned and hiked a leg up onto a low branch.

"What the hell are you doing? Get down before you get us thrown out of here."

He climbed toward a narrow spread between two branches. "I hid the picnic basket up here. I balanced the wicker perfectly between two branches, and the leaves kept it hidden from sight."

"You do realize I wasn't talking about actual lunch, right?" She held her arms up, taking the basket as he lowered it toward the ground.

Jumping from the branches, he landed with barely a sound on the balls of his feet like a sexy, modern day Robin Hood. "If you were, I'd have changed your mind with a single kiss."

She rested the basket against the tree and then looked at him dryly. "And what makes you so sure you could change my mind? You've never seen me when I'm hangry. It's scary."

"Hangry," he repeated. "As in so hungry you'll rip someone a new one until they feed you?"

"Pretty much."

He strode toward her, walking her backwards until her back pressed against the tree. With both palms on the rough bark, he leaned in, letting the promise of a kiss hover above her lips.

"So, are you planning on feeding me or what?"

"Depends. I've seen you so starved you would have begged if I let you. But I'm such a nice guy, I didn't make you wait too long for *satisfaction*."

He traced the seam of her lips with the tip of his tongue, pulling back when she opened for a kiss. "I think you want me to make you beg. I think you want a mouthwatering, torturous wait before I feed you inches."

Her body hummed, and her panties were soaked at just his words. The thought of teasing

torment, building until she clawed for release left her breathless.

She ached for him, yet he held himself in check, even as her chest heaved close enough to feel her heart pound.

"Fuck the risk." She licked her lips, straining for his mouth. "I want you here and now, Gareth."

He shook his head, leaving her panting as he moved to lift the lid to the picnic basket.

Food? He got her all hot and bothered and he'd rather eat a drumstick?

Rummaging underneath the Tupperware, he pulled out a nylon bag. "I told you this was a surprise."

With a sexy half grin, he untied the drawstring top and pulled a tiny dildo from the bag. "What do you think, Goldilocks? Hmmm? Methinks this one is too small and too soft."

He put it back in the bag with a wink before pulling another out with a flourish.

"Gareth, what the—" Lane's eyes went wide at the giant horse cock dildo in his hand.

"Too scary? Even for a hangry girl like you?" He tsked. "Well, perhaps this one *is* too big and too hard."

"Oh my God. You're nuts! What if they searched the whole picnic basket at the entrance?"

He pressed a finger to his lips and reached into the bag for a third time. "Let's see." Pulling a third

dildo out, he palmed the synthetic flesh before walking with it to where Lane stood flabbergasted. "I think this one is just right. Don't you?"

His free hand reached for her breast as he pressed the realistic silicone into her palm. "This one is just the right length. The right girth. Smooth, yet fleshy and hard."

Taking her free hand, he pressed it to the hard bar behind his fly. "Almost like the real thing."

Lane gasped as his cock jerked behind the soft denim. She'd had him so many times before, but never enough.

"Tell me, Laney. Which would you rather suck? My thick meat or the thick silicone in your hand? Maybe you'll give me a smokin' hot visual and tongue them both."

Her heart jackhammered in her chest so hard she could barely form words. "The wards."

"I placed wards when I put the basket here. We'll have to strengthen them, but to do so we need to raise your power, and the only way to do that is for me to make you come."

She couldn't think as he lifted the hem of her spring dress, running his fingers between her legs.

"You're so wet, love. I can feel your slick sex through your panties and your clit is throbbing."

He slid the tips of his fingers under the top lace band and over her damp mound. "Against the tree,

no one will see you groan and clench as my fingers work your wet slit."

He spread her slick folds, curling his hand deep. Two fingers, then three. Lane moaned at the rough feel, her breath catching when he circled her clit with his thumb, pumping his hand slowly.

Pinned against the trunk, Lane struggled for traction, trying to grind her sex deeper, harder into Gareth's hand.

He took her mouth, teasing her tongue and her lips with gentle kisses to match the gentle strokes on her pussy.

"Gareth!" she ground out.

He smiled against her lips. "I'm feeding your hunger, love, but obviously it's not enough. What do you want?"

A choked moan left her throat, raw and low.

"Say the words, Lane."

Jaw tight, she exhaled. "More, Gareth! I want more! Hard. Deep. I need it! Give it to me, please!"

Taking the dildo from her hand, he slid it between them, but she stopped his hand. Shaking her head, she held his wrist off.

"I want more, but I want *you*. Not synthetic flesh. *Your* flesh. I want you to fill me. Your cock. Your cum. In me now."

She took the dildo from him and tossed it toward the bag on the grass, not caring who saw or who came.

Gareth's eyes never left her hungry gaze as he unbuttoned his fly, freeing his member. Lifting her hips, he pushed her back against the tree, spreading her wide. Lane locked her ankles around his back, and he impaled her slick flesh with a single thrust.

Driving his hard length balls deep, she ignored the sting of the rough bark through her top. There was nothing gentle or slow now.

Gareth buried his head in the hollow of her neck, kissing her throat and the tender flesh of her jaw as he drove higher, deeper. He found her mouth and crushed his lips to hers, devouring her lips and tongue.

Their auras tingled, merging and flooding in and around their entwined bodies. Gold sparkles glinted as power rose between them and through them the closer they climbed toward climax.

With a sharp breath, he tore his mouth from hers. "My cock is ready to blow. Quickly, Lane! Reach for the knife in my back pocket. It's time!"

Not knowing what he meant, she fumbled blindly, sliding her fingers into the denim slit. Finding it, she wrapped her hand around the shaft and pulled it free.

Small enough to fit in the palm of her hand, she blinked at the ornate lettering on the handle.

"Open it and cut my palm. Do the same on your hand. The same as we did at the Red Veil."

"Why?"

His voice shook and sweat broke out on his forehead. "Do it, Lane!"

Every muscle in his body went rigid, so she dragged the sharp tip across his palm the same as she did the previous night.

"Now you. You have to trust me."

She did as he asked, and Gareth took her hand, pressing palm to palm. His leaned in, pressing his forehead to hers. His warm, sweet breath tickled her nose and mouth, and it tasted of power, of magic. Like honey sizzling on the tongue.

He pulled back, and his eyes found hers and locked. *"Root of my root, star spun lives. Bound in flesh and spirit light. Blood of my blood, bone of my bone, I claim thee now as we are one. United in life, transcended in death, the claim is cast on Danu's breath."*

Their blood flowed together, and his words teemed in her mind, expanding, shimmering like the golden force surrounding them.

Magic hummed in the air and in their flesh. Lane held tight as they spun, the world falling away. Body light, she floated with senses on fire.

Gareth filled her body and soul, and with a cry everything swelled. They moved together, seamless, boneless, climbing higher and higher until sheer power overwhelmed, and they exploded, climaxing into spasms.

Magic flowed, a river encircling them, pulling them under until it ebbed, leaving them panting as they clung together, the world returning.

Lane opened her eyes, expecting to see the earth spinning below then, only to find the sun winking through the leaves and her back still pressed against the bark.

Gareth lifted his head, still clasping their joined hands. "You okay?"

She exhaled a stunned breath. "Okay? What the hell was that?"

He let go of her hand and she jerked it close to see what caused such a tumult. "What the—"

The cut had healed, and in its place a white scar had formed at the center of her palm. Not a thin line as expected, but an intricate Celtic knot intertwined with the symbols for love and eternity.

"Don't worry. I have one, too." Gareth held up his hand. "It's a claiming sigil. It means you're safe now, no matter which plane we decide to roam."

She shoved at his shoulder. "Claiming sigil?!"

"Laney, you agreed. In the library, remember?"

"In the library? That was last night, Gareth! You could have warned me that's what was happening. I thought we died or something!"

He gaped. "More like died and gone to heaven. That was the single most intense sexual experience of my life. I can't believe you're saying it wasn't the same for you."

This time she punched his shoulder. "I never said it wasn't! It was fucking amazing. Fourth of July, Yule and Halloween all rolled into one. Fireworks and starbursts. But YOU SHOULD HAVE TOLD ME!"

"You agreed. Caitlan told you. The only way you'd be safe from Leith's master plan was for you to be claimed. You seemed thrilled when you realized she meant me. Happy even."

She exhaled. "I didn't say I wasn't. It's just—I would have liked to have been ready."

He laughed, pecking her lips with a quick kiss. "Trust me, love. You were *more* than ready. Dripping ready. It wouldn't have happened if you weren't. As for what to expect, how would I know?" He shrugged. "I've never claimed a mate before, so how could I tell you what would happen when I didn't have a clue?"

"Asking for a heads up in this isn't like ruining a surprise birthday party. It's a claiming. You could have warned me you were going to perform the rite. You knew the words. You must have looked them up or something."

"Those words aren't written anywhere except my heart. The only thing necessary for a claiming is sexual climax and the words, 'I claim.'" He shrugged. "The rest was all me." Taking her hand, his gaze dropped before he looked up again. "I'm sorry, Laney. I should have told you what I

planned. I suppose I wanted it to knock your socks off."

Lane's heart squeezed. Gareth was her equal in everything. Her lover, her friend, her partner in crime and everything in between. How could she hold a Type A personality against him when she was the same? His actions and his words reflected something so beautiful, so surprisingly tender, and the feeling behind them far outweighed the rest.

"I'm sorry, too, Gareth."

"Sorry we're mated, or sorry for being such a pig-headed Raven about it?"

She punched his shoulder again.

"Hey! Ouch!"

"You knew what you were getting when you signed up for this rollercoaster. No backsies. I'm yours and you're mine. End of sentence. Just promise me you'll give me a heads-up next time something important happens that affects us both."

He kissed the end of her nose. "Deal."

"Good. Now let's get cleaned up before we really get arrested."

He stepped back, letting his still thick member slide from her body before gently helping her to the ground. "Careful, Lane. Get your legs first."

"*Oomph*." She wobbled, holding on to his arm. "You're not kidding. That was really one wild ride, Mr. Toad."

"Please tell me you are not telling Caitlan to turn me into an amphibian simply because I claimed you sort of on the sly."

She laughed, snorting a little. "No, dummy. It's the Disney classic. *Mr. Toad's Wild Ride?*"

He shook his head.

"You have so been gone from this plane for too long. Once this is over, we are taking a trip to Orlando and the Magic Kingdom."

"Sounds like just the place for two Fae halflings."

Once she found her feet, she turned, showing him her back. "How chewed up are my shoulders and my dress?"

"Not at all, why?" He brushed a little crushed bark from her dress.

"I thought I'd be a scraped, bloody mess for sure."

He grinned, pulling Tupperware out of the picnic basket to hide the sex bag underneath. "We need to get back and fill Caitlan in on what happened, and then get the vampires onboard."

"Wait." She bent, stopping him from packing the food again. "There's hungry and then there's *hungry*. This is forever *our* spot, so why not spread the picnic blanket under our tree and enjoy the sunshine? Caitlan can wait. We joined ourselves in front of nature and the whole universe. I think this

calls for a little happy before the hell begins, don't you?"

He straightened, pulling her into his arms. "Never a little happy. All happy. All the time."

Chapter Fifteen

"Y ou sure Caitlan filled the vampires in on everything? What about the three rogue fangers involved in this mess?" Gareth asked, checking his watch again.

"She told them the whole story. In fact, she said they were already well aware of what happened on that macabre merry-go-round."

He exhaled a dubious breath. "I hope they're coming to help, and not just to take their pound of Fae flesh. Vampires are fickle, yet exacting creatures. In the absence of the true culprit, guilt by blood association suffices for them. I hope Caitlan took that into account when she arranged for us to meet them here of all places."

"If concrete could talk," Gareth added with a low breath, glancing at the stained walls outside the side entrance to the Red Veil.

Lane followed his line of sight. The discolorations on the wall and the asphalt below could be anything, but the look on Gareth's face wasn't wrong. It could be old blood. "I doubt we were asked here for a nefarious reason. The

vampires specified this entrance because it's the only way into the Red Veil during the day. The others are sealed off for obvious reasons."

"Considering how much time you've spent here, if anyone knows the odd hours kept by the undead, it's you."

Lane's brows knotted at the obvious dig. "Wow. Snarky much? I thought you said my time here was a turn on."

"I did. And I meant it. But I'm back now, so—" He shrugged off the last bit as if it was taken as fact.

With a hand on her hip, Lane raised an eyebrow. "So, you're insinuating it's no longer acceptable for me to come here because you're back. Is that the subtext of what you just said?"

"I didn't say that."

"Good. Because if that's what you meant, I might have to practice my dick shriveling spells on your private parts." She looked at him, hoping the attempt at levity defused a potential argument.

"Gareth, picking up where we left off ten years ago is one thing, but regardless of how we still feel about each other, we've grown as people. If we have any hope of going forward, you have to accept I'm not the naïve headstrong girl I once was. I'm an adult, with ten years of living without you. I never was, nor am I now, the kind who likes to be told what I can and cannot do. Now…" she moved to put her hand on his arm. "If you meant you're back,

and that you'd like to accompany me to the backrooms whenever the urge presents, that's another story."

He grumbled a response, and Lane bit the inside of her cheek not to laugh. Gareth may have come into his Fae power, but he was still Gareth when it came to her. Gorgeous, eager, and altogether endearing for being such a caveman, sometimes. Not that she'd ever tell him. Still, she was as much an alpha female as he was alpha male, and it made for interesting sparks all the way around.

"We should be meeting up at the Botanical Gardens. That's ground zero for us." He crossed his arms. "Hells bells, do you know how long it'll take us to get to the Bronx from lower Manhattan?"

At his ruffled posturing, she stifled a smirk and let her hand drop from his arm. "My guess is not that long, considering the time of night and the fact certain vampires can fly."

"Fly?" With a disbelieving look, he put up two hands. "Hell no. Undead Uber is not happening tonight."

She cracked a smile. "Whichever way we get there, I'm sure it'll be fine."

Mollified, his forehead relaxed, and he loosened the vise grip on his arms. "I shouldn't be so cynical about the fanged set. You're right. They have a stake in this, too."

"Hey, that was my pun." The smile on her face faded after a moment. "All joking aside. My Spidey senses are buzzing, but it's not from the vampires. I can't help but feel the fates are fucking with us from a distance. Maybe that's what you're picking up on."

"Fucking with us how?"

Lane lifted an uncertain hand. "I'm not sure, but something's blindsiding us. I can taste it."

"Because the Rose Garden is under renovation and closed to the public?" he asked. "We knew this was going to be tricky, Laney, but to be honest, all that tarpaulin blanketing the gazebo at the site might be a good thing. It gives us cover. Besides, every lesser Fae in that garden knows we're here. I caught them peeping at us all this afternoon. Even at the most inopportune moments, if you get my drift."

His look left no room for guessing, and she had to laugh. "Peeping. As in Peeping Toms?"

"More like Peeping Pixies, and brownies, and even a few phookas. At least I didn't sense any boggarts or sluagh. Gnarly buggers. The idea of those ill-begotten creatures watching us have sex is enough to cause erectile disfunction. We should be glad they don't show much during the day."

She burst out laughing. "Sloo-ah? That sounds like something you hack up after a chest cold."

"They're haggard and ugly, so you're not that far off. They usually skulk in the shadows and have been known to be the eyes and ears for the Dark Court, but the truth is they're more mercenary than that. Their aim is ripping souls from unsuspecting humans."

"Wonderful. The idea of Faerie just keeps getting better and better." She paused. "Wait. If they're mercenary, then they can be bought."

He nodded. "Exactly. While commerce with the Sluagh is always distasteful, it might come in handy at some point. And since the undead involved are at the mercy of a dark Sidhe, meeting the Sluagh's price might be an ace up our sleeve."

"I don't know, Gareth. I'd rather not bargain like that with Eve at stake. Or me for that matter. I'd like to keep my soul intact."

Shrugging, he checked his watch again. "Then we'll let the vampires negotiate with them if necessary. They're soulless, so it won't be an issue. I think we need to rally all supernatural species involved. Strength in paranormal numbers."

"I couldn't agree more, but I do argue the point that the undead are soulless. We are, in fact, not so."

Gareth wheeled around, instinctively pushing Lane behind him. Standing in the shadows across from them was an imposing vampire. Mysteriously beautiful, with long gold hair and one side of his face ruined.

"I apologize for startling you. Allow me to introduce myself. I am Rémy Tessier. Elder, and acting head of the Vampire Council. You must be Gareth Fairfax and Lane Alden, Fae halflings."

An elegant female vampire approached, rounding the corner as Rémy finished his introduction. "Ah, good. Right on time, as usual," Rémy said, lifting a hand to her.

The vampire smoothed the front of her vintage Chanel suit before moving to where Rémy stood with two strangers. She got within five feet of them and stopped. "Witch!" Her eyes flared crimson and her fangs descended.

Rémy's hand shot forward, grabbing her before she attacked. "Abigail, let me introduce our *guests*." He stressed the word. "Lane Arden and Gareth Fairfax. True, they are witches, but they are also Ravens."

She blinked, her eyes narrowing. "Ravens, as in the *Circle of the Raven*. As in Fae-kissed?"

He inclined his head. "Yes. They are halfling Fae to be precise, and they're here to help with this unfortunate situation. It seems an initiate of the motherhouse was taken last night from the Red Veil. The unfortunate Were we found dead was used to draw her to the backrooms. We believe the act was premeditated."

"Premeditated?" she questioned. "Bette told me the Were in question was found drained in the

Carousel room. If he was part of a planned conspiracy, then why is he dead?" Abigail looked at the two witches.

"I saw what happened to him," Lane replied. "I don't mean I witnessed his death firsthand. I have second sight. I can't tell you much about him, other than his name was Mason. He was supposed to be a one-night stand for a stressed-out student." She looked to Rémy. "I'm sorry, but I have to agree with your vampire friend. I don't see how Mason was a part of this. Eve used a compulsion spell on him, so he'd take particular interest in her."

Abigail exhaled a cutting breath.

Lane turned an arched brow at the elegant, strawberry blonde vampire. "You sound as though you object. Don't vamps glamour their victims into exposing arteries and genitals and whatever else catches your fancy?"

She took it one step farther, sparing a look for Gareth. "Maybe we Ravens should leave the undead out of this completely and report the incident to the Alpha of the Brethren. Sean Leighton is a good friend of our Supreme. I'm sure he'd be interested to hear what happened to one of his own at the club *you* run."

"Lane—" Gareth's tone was a warning.

She lifted a hand. "No, it's okay. The undead are used to being at the top of the food chain. So, having wards they raised crumble at our fingertips,

and their refuge infiltrated, must be upsetting. But we're not the ones they should be scrutinizing. Three of their own are at the heart of how this happened on their turf, so, Abigail…physician, heal thyself."

Bette joined them at that moment, rounding the corner the same way Abigail came. "What do doctors have to do with any of this?" she asked, stopping beside Rémy on the other side.

"It's Shakespeare, love," Gareth replied, keeping an eye on both Lane and Abigail.

"Lane is correct," Rémy replied with a wave, signaling Abigail to stand down. "We need to look within to find the guilty parties."

Gareth shook his head. "Not guilty. Just answerable."

"I think the witchy dude has a point," Bette chimed in, gesturing toward Gareth.

"Gareth," he said, giving her a quick nod.

"Go on," Rémy prompted Bette. "Have you pinpointed anyone from the work rota?"

She paused before bobbing her head. "Yes, but I also agree with Gareth. The undead involved were compelled, and a single vampire couldn't inflict the number of bite wounds we saw on that luckless Were. It has to be more than one."

"There were three vampires, to be exact," Lane interjected, keeping one eye on Abigail. "I saw

them when I touched the restraints on the chair across from the carousel."

"Psychometry?" Rémy questioned.

Lane nodded. "It's a form of ESP, but in this instance, the residual energy was so thick I could taste it."

"Literally," Gareth added. "It made her retch."

Bette nodded, making a face. "I felt it, too. Not in the same way, but it was profound."

"Anyway," Abigail redirected. "We have been on high alert since the breach. I reviewed the tapes from the night in question. The Carousel Room, to be exact. We know who of our kind was involved, how long they stayed, and when they left."

"So, you knew all along who was involved?" Lane took a step forward.

"Sorry, I'm late. The city is packed with tourists tonight." They all turned toward Caitlan joining them from the street.

The Supreme's voice stopped Lane in her tracks, and she moved back to Gareth's side, ignoring the smirk on Abigail's face.

"Sean Leighton has been made aware of the situation, now that we're all on the same page," Caitlan continued. "He asked that the Raven motherhouse be permitted to deal with our issues first, before the vampires enact their justice. He also asked that Rémy contact him afterward, considering how and where Mason met his end."

"Agreed." Gareth nodded. "First things first."

Abigail balked. "First things first? Your kind *caused* the breach in the first place. Witches and Fae are forbidden entry into the Red Veil, yet you chose to use your powers to circumvent that rule. We are only here because your Supreme requested our presence, plus we need to see for ourselves the Fae responsible is taken to task."

"You can bet your sweet fangs, sister," Gareth replied. "The Sidhe responsible for this will die."

"Kill him if you must," Abigail added, but then spared a sly smile for Rémy and Bette. "But there are other, more satisfying ways to exact retribution."

Caitlan shook her head, in effect wiping the smirk from Abigail's face. "This particular Fae needs to die, and by Lane's hand. Besides, it's too dangerous for you to keep a Fae on tap, literally—and from the way your master is nodding, I can safely assume he agrees. I also believe the Alpha of the Brethren will want both Lane and Gareth at the sit down between the Weres and the vampires, once our business with this rogue Sidhe is concluded. After all, they were the ones who discovered Mason's body, and tracked the images and scents to the culprits."

"Indeed," Rémy agreed. "You'll have to forgive my indulgences. Abigail's heart may be silent, but it is in the right place when it comes to our kind.

She is as protective of our own as you are of yours, and this situation has not presented her character in the best light. She is not as callous as she seems.

"In fact, she has learned tolerance beyond what most vampires are capable, especially in overcoming past taboos. I let her have her head at times, but in this case, I think it best to defer to you." He inclined his head. "Madame Raven, the Vampire Council of New York is at your disposal."

Chapter Sixteen

"*D*amn it! My pants are soaked to my knees!" Gareth grumbled as he climbed onto the east bank of the Bronx River. "Ugh, and I stink. That water is filthy, polluted."

Lane chuckled. "Be grateful Bette waited for you take your shoes off."

"I don't think that youngblood has full powers of flight. I'm lucky she didn't drop me at the deepest point."

Lane brushed off her pants before smoothing her hair back into a long ponytail. "Ha! That would have been practically unintentional."

"No thanks to you and your top of the food chain remarks." Gareth snorted.

She grinned, watching him squeeze out his pant cuffs. "Yet she somehow managed to place me on dry land."

"Beginner's luck."

"At least Rémy made Abigail stay behind with Caitlan. Things were starting to get ugly."

"Starting?" He laughed. "We're lucky Abigail can't fly, or she'd have dropped us onto the nearest

garbage barge. If what Rémy said about vampires overcoming taboos is correct, your mouth single handedly set things back to naught."

"I did not," she shot back, reaching for the penlight and map in her back pocket.

"How far are we to the Rose Garden from here?"

Lane glanced past her shoulder into the gloom. "About twenty minutes via that path." She put the flashlight in her teeth, shining the soft yellow light on the map. "I know we agreed it's the fastest way, but now I think we should keep to the trees along the perimeter."

She traced the red outline on the map indicating a copse of cherry trees and then lilacs closer to the Rose Garden.

"We might run into lesser Fae there, but we should be fine," Gareth replied. "I wasn't able to learn much about the park's night security other than they patrol every hour or so. We didn't breach the fence, and there's really no buildings other than the greenhouse and one staff building, but I don't want to push our luck until we're at the site and can throw up a ward."

A whoosh caught their attention and they turned to see Rémy land soundlessly on the opposite bank across the water. With a single leap, he crossed to their embankment, walking with sure grace to where they stood waiting. "Caitlan

thought you might need a hand keeping unwanted observers at bay."

Gareth grinned. "As long as you promise not to make a midnight snack out of the lesser Fae who reside in the gardens. If you get peckish, you can have the security detail."

The three kept to the shadows and the soft spring grass. The night was cool, but it had lost the winter chill that sometimes lingered in the early spring. Instead, there was a sweetness to the air that tasted of rebirth and the promise of summer.

"Rémy, what did you mean about Abigail and overcoming past taboos?" Lane asked, breaking their silence.

He considered her for a moment. "Abigail is superior, haughty. Impeccable in manner and dress, but ruthless in her desires. She was our former master's progeny, and his envoy before he fell from grace. When he met his final death from his own actions during the HepZ outbreak, it was hard on her.

"Then she met a shifter named Dash Collier. He headed the contingent of Weres the Alpha of the Brethren sent to help clear our shadow houses of the virus. Whatever Abigail threw at him...insults, jibes, even sex, he met her headstrong and head on. She had finally met her match.

"As you probably know, Weres and Vampires are natural enemies. Fraternization was taboo on

both sides for centuries, until we needed each other in order to survive. In the aftermath of all that death, old prejudices no longer made sense. Abigail and Dash were the first to realize that and have been happy together since.

"You see, taboos are crumbling everywhere in our shared shadowed world. It's why I have chosen not to indict your breach at the Red Veil, despite Abigail's protest. It is true witch blood poses a problem for us, and Abigail's resentment stems from more than one undead friend meeting an ugly death because it. Even if those friends weren't discerning or careful about where or on whom they fed.

"Even with the risk, I'm willing to take the chance on a truce. And so is your Supreme. It's why I agreed to come with you tonight. With the right measures, I'm hopeful we can find a way to manage the situation, much in the same way the Weres manage theirs when it comes to vampire blood."

Blunt guilt slashed at Lane for jumping to earlier conclusions and she pursed her lips, watching the elegant predator move beside them with ease.

"You are obviously a remarkable man, Rémy Tessier," she offered. "I owe you an apology."

He grinned, and a hint of fang glinted in the moonlight. "So, you're putting us back at the top of the food chain then, eh?"

"Don't push it." She chuckled.

"And on that note, we're halfway there." Gareth stopped on the grass separating the copse of cherry trees from the early blooming lilacs. "We can either cut through here or veer over toward the path and bluestone circle just above the Rockefeller Rose Garden."

The full moon illuminated the small grove where they stood, and the grassy trail that cut through to Rose Garden. The labyrinth of gorgeous rose bushes was muted in the moonlight, as was the gazebo at the center of the lush landscaped architecture, covered in a dull green tarpaulin.

"Why risk the pavement when we're so close?" Lane gestured toward the soft slope ahead.

Gareth shrugged, non-committal. "It's six- and one-half dozen of another to me, but I thought you might want a break from the damp grass."

Together they moved toward the fragrant trees, but Rémy stayed put, motionless.

"Rémy? Is everything all right?" Lane asked.

"Something is barring my entry."

Before she could ask another question, a dull wince creased the vampire's face. "It's warded. With *Ferfaen*. The druid's plant."

"No unclean shall pass," a growly rasp croaked from the shadows. "How dare you bring an unclean to befoul our garden."

The rough voice came from the shadows, and Lane threw a hand outward, speaking a druid word for light. "*Soilsigh!*"

The little beast hissed, clamoring back into shadow, but not before they saw its squat, thickset body covered with matted hair. Eyes blinked at them, glowing red and saucer-like in the refracted light.

Long prominent teeth showed behind thin lips, and skinny fingers armed with talons shielded its face.

"What manner of beast is this?" Rémy asked, taking a step closer to the creature only to have it hiss again. "If it thinks I'm unclean, then it hasn't looked in the mirror lately."

"Looks to be half boggart, half hogboon. Nasty mischief-maker mixed with a sweet-natured goblin," Gareth answered.

"A sweet goblin?" Rémy peered even closer. "Sounds like an oxymoron."

The creature snorted. "Ye thinks ye better? Ye defile the garden with yer unclean self. Begone! Before ye hurt more!"

"Hurt?" Gareth questioned, only to hear a clipped growl for an answer.

The creature scuttled forward, teeth bared, stopping short only when Lane stepped in front of both Gareth and Rémy.

"*Princesssss!*"

Its protracted hiss at the end of the word made her teeth hurt. "Who are you?" she questioned, raising another light spiral in her hand just in case.

"I be Xax, and I speak for the wee folk here. We folk mind our own, but ye and yers think it fun to hurt us for sport. Ye had yer help before, but don't think to be trolling for blood here anymore, missy. We banished the Redcaps when they chose the bloodsucking unclean that came with the new king. They've dipped their caps in our life's blood for the last time. You'll find no quarter and no help here."

Pixies divebombed like marauding flies, as two grimy-haired boggarts and a stray phooka came into view.

"*Jesus*, they're like a swarm on crack!" Gareth batted them away, but there were always more. "Ouch! They've got knives! Fucking mosquitos with swords!"

They didn't go near Rémy, but Lane ducked and twisted, waving her hands to fend them off as well.

With a wince, Rémy moved to Lane's side and the attack stopped immediately. He flicked one from Lane's shoulder with his thumb and forefinger. "Unclean, one. Psycho Tinkerbelle, zip."

A low moan caught Lane's attention and she turned toward the pained sound. She spoke the word for light again, only this time it showed a smaller version of Xax. A female, and she was injured.

Lane took a step toward the injured lesser, and Xax shot forward, blocking her way. "*Princesssss*, show mercy. I beg ye!"

The ugly belligerent creature was obviously the wounded lesser Fae's mate. Lane looked from him to Gareth. "Leith must have convinced these outcasts he defeated the Unseelie king and took over the court. That's what he meant by new king."

Her voice never moved above a whisper, but Xax heard her, nonetheless. He pulled himself to his full height, all two feet of him, and sniffed. "We be exiles, not outcasts. Thrown from our home in the roses because of the likes of ye and ye father."

"Leith is my father, but I'm no princess, and neither is he king," Lane replied. "The Unseelie king still rules. Leith is a liar and a murdering bastard, and he not only interacts with the unclean," she shot Rémy an apologetic look, "but he has them do his bidding against you and others of our kind."

The creature spit, and its saliva sizzled on the pavement leaving a pitted black spot. "A curse on his name!"

"Answer us this. Why can't our friend pass? Is the ground spelled?" Lane demanded.

The hogboon halfling turned with another sniff toward the shadows, clearly unwilling to play.

"Okay, Xax. I've got something for you, but only if you play nice." Lane dug in the canvas bag

hanging across her chest, pulling out a handful of dollar store Marti Gras beads.

The creature turned, and eyes went wide as it stared at the colorful costume beads. Its thin lips parted, and it took an absent step forward.

Gareth looked at Lane. "Seriously?"

"When you said lesser Fae might live in the Gardens, I did a little research. Brownies and pixies like milk, phookas and boggarts like crops, goblins like shiny objects, especially jewelry."

"For Xax, *princesssss*?" The creature asked, pointing to his hairy chest.

She nodded. Opening her bag, she fished out an ear of corn and a container of heavy cream, placing all the offerings at the base of a lilac tree. "I have more, but I want answers."

They clamored for the offerings, sparing the three of them furtive looks before moving toward the shadows again.

"Wait," Lane stopped the goblin. "Why is my friend barred from the trees?"

The creature showed a wide set of long sharp teeth in a grotesque smile. "Because I warded his ilk, after those with the king hurt my Eesa. Ferfaen brewed thick and rich, and then poured into the earth that none who feed from living blood may pass."

"Eesa?" she questioned.

The hogboon goblin nodded once, and his red eyes seemed wet. "My mate." Xax lifted a clawed hand toward the injured female. "They found her in the roses gathering nectar, and they dragged her into—"

The little creature's voice cracked, and Rémy stopped him from explaining further. There was no need. The heartbreak on his face said it all.

With a hand on his heart, the vampire stepped forward and knelt to one knee. "Those that hurt your mate will be punished. You have my word."

"Are ye their king?" Xax's wide red eyes searched his for the truth.

Nodding, Rémy bowed his head and the hogboon goblin sniffed, giving him a nod back.

Waving a skinny, taloned hand, the ward barring Rémy from the grove crumbled with a low bell-like tinkle. Xax lifted a clawed finger and pointed it at the vampire. "Ye may pass, but ye won't enter the roses. The *princesssss* and her mate be the only two."

Rémy straightened, stalemated. "I'm out of my element here. Looks like you're on your own from this point. I'll do what I can from this side, but I cannot help if you get caught within."

"Salt and light," Gareth offered. "That should keep this lot at bay if they get too curious. Not that it's likely. The best thing you can do for us is keep

unwanted human visitors away so we can do what we came to do."

"The false king expects ye through the roses," Xax interrupted. "He has one like ye. He feeds from her." The hogboon's chin dropped to his chest before he met Lane's eyes. "A friend, I think. She waits for ye to come."

Gareth put a staying hand on Lane's arm. "If Leith is expecting us through the roses, then the gazebo is a trap. There has to be another way."

"Xax will take ye through the tunnels."

Lane turned on her heel to watch Eesa struggle to stand.

"Eesa, no. It is forbidden."

"Xax," she coughed, "ye must take them. If the false king did this to us, what will he do to all the others?"

Lane dumped the contents of her bag at Xax's feet. "I'll bring you sacks of shiny jewels and as much cream as you can drink, if you can help us find a way to defeat the false king."

His saucer red eyes blinked, and when he cocked his head to watch her face, he looked like a demented cross between Dobby and a Gringotts's goblin from *Harry Potter*.

"The false king is yer father. How can we trust ye?"

Eesa coughed again as one of the boggarts helped her rest on a soft tuft of grass, and the small female's face winced with the effort.

"Gareth, can halfling Sidhe use their light to heal?"

He shook his head. "As far and I know, our magic is for defense and attack."

"Halflings might not be able to heal the small one, but I can." At Rémy's announcement, the grove went quiet.

Xax craned his neck to look at the tall vampire. His lips pulled back over his teeth in warning.

"*Uhm*, maybe that's not such a great idea right now," Gareth cautioned. "You're not exactly supernatural species of the month."

Rémy ignored him, taking a tentative step toward the hogboon goblin. Xax raised his hand, and blue magic sparked deadly. The energy bomb flew without warning and Rémy blurred out of the way.

The attack shattered a small bounder, sending rock shrapnel flying and the lesser Fae running for cover.

"Holy crap!" Lane and Gareth dove for the nearest tree.

Gareth covered her with his body as residual energy snapped and fizzed. "Goblins are no joke. They have abilities innate to their breed and pack quite a punch."

"I know you have no reason to trust me or my nature, but I speak the truth," Rémy tried again. "I promised with bent knee I would see justice done for you and your mate. She suffered when her blood was taken, and only fate knows what else."

"Do not speak of it! Ye lips are not worthy."

Gareth peeked his head around to watch the hogboon ready with another bomb. "Hang on, love."

Another ball grew in the hogboon goblin's hand.

"Vampires take blood, it's true." He ran for a tree, sparks singeing his cloak before the sizzling ball exploded in the grass where he last stood.

"But it's also true we have the power to heal!" Rémy lifted a surrendering hand and stepped from cover into the open. "I'm done running from you. As an elder, I take responsibility for the actions of the undead that hurt your mate. Attack if you must, but I'm telling you now my blood can heal. Will heal."

Xax's ears flicked and his red eyes narrowed, but the tilt of his head showed he was listening.

"Even a few drops will replenish and do no harm."

Eesa coughed again, struggling to sit up. "Xax, let him approach."

The hogboon looked from her to the vampire, uncertainty warring on his face with the need to protect.

"I will not touch her, if that is your wish. Eesa can take a few drops from my wrist directly onto her tongue."

Eesa winced, beckoning them both, and Xax glanced to the other lesser Fae before giving Rémy a nod.

The elder vampire knelt beside the small female. Using his thumbnail, he pierced the vein in his wrist and held it over her mouth.

The little hogboon goblin hesitated at first, but then licked her cracked lips as blood droplets fell. She grasped hold of Rémy's wrist and licked the wound, drinking directly from his vein until he gently moved her back.

Her ashen skin now held a lush brown sheen, and her flesh plumped. Dull eyes shined bright red with flecks of green and she took her first easy breath. Holding her hand out to Xax, he helped her to her feet.

"Thank ye," he said, offering the elder vampire a stocky bow.

Eesa tapped him on the shoulder and then pointed toward a nondescript boulder at the edge of the lilac grove.

He nodded, and then closed his eyes for a moment. When he opened them again, he lifted his

mate's hand to his formidable mouth. He kissed her knuckles, and then wrapped his long, clawed fingers around her hand.

"Come." He gestured for Lane and Gareth to follow. Sparing a look for Rémy, he placed a fist over his heart.

Rémy copied the move. "Don't worry, my warrior friend. I will protect your mate and your friends until you return. Those that did this to you will meet their final death either by my hand, or by the hand of the Fae halfling at your side. Though I hope she saves the honor for me."

"If I can, I will," Lane replied, tapping the canvas bag strapped across her chest.

"Godspeed…*princesssss*." Rémy winked, mimicking the hogboon goblin's speech, and he and the lesser Fae watched the three disappear into the unknown.

Chapter Seventeen

"*A* concealed portal right in the middle of a State Park." Lane watched as Xax cut a narrow ribbon in the shimmering membrane warding the entry from prying eyes.

The jagged edge of the rock face seemed monolithic in size and shape, and she wondered if it was naturally occurring or if the *Cinn ag Taitneamh* had placed it here by design.

A crack spread, wide enough for a man to squeeze past sideways, and Xax stepped through the opening first. When he gave the signal, he stepped to the side, allowing Lane and Gareth to follow.

Lane's skin tingled as she stepped through the entry and her body shivered. Once through, she wiped her arms and legs with her palms, smoothing her hair as if a film had somehow stuck.

"Ew, that's got to be by design," she said, wiggling around.

"Lane, what the hell are you doing?"

She made a face, still smoothing her hair. "You don't feel that?"

"Feel what? The transition?"

"Is that what you call it? God, it's like walking through a spider's web, soft but instinctively icky. Man, if the wards don't stop you, that creep factor totally does the trick."

He laughed. "You'll get used to it."

"Ugh, no thanks."

The hogboon goblin turned, lifting a hand to the crevice from the inside to begin the incantation to close the portal.

"Xax, don't. Leave it open for now."

His ears flicked. "I cannot. Ye can't enter further into the Middle Course if the portal be open to the human plane."

"Middle Course?"

Xax bobbed his furry head. "Yes, mistress. Be what this is. Middle Course. Neither Earth nor Faerie. It be in between."

"Xax, I understand your predicament, and we appreciate everything you've done for us so far, but if you close the rock portal and we get separated or something untoward happens, Lane and I will be trapped."

Gareth swung an arm toward the myriad tunnels facing them ahead. Xax seemed to consider his point, his red eyes gleaming in the semi-dark.

For a moment his eyes flickered orange and then he smiled a sharp-toothed grin. "Do ye know the *Ballad of Tam Lin*? Tis a long poem."

"Yes, why?" Gareth nodded, but raised an eyebrow at the odd question.

"Have ye a silver blade? Best with runes and sigils."

Gareth nodded, sparing a perplexed look for Lane.

The hogboon goblin tapped the side of his heart-shaped head. "Clever it is, and magic it holds. Say the final lines of the lament and trace a five-pointed star in the air. Any portal ye want will open." He nodded, giggling to himself. "Tis Goblin magic so be afeared. The portal once opened can suck ye straight through to the other side and keep ye hostage. Tricky it be but use if ye must."

Xax then closed the rock portal and then turned with a little skip. Since they entered the Middle Course, the little hogboon had energy and his skin seemed to glow even in the dim light.

"You like it here, Xax?" Lane asked.

He bobbed his head, holding his palm toward a wall torch. The end flamed immediately, and Xax motioned for Gareth to take it.

"All Fae folk take sustenance of spirit from Fae-kissed ground. The Middle Course is as close as we exiled can be to our home."

The tunnels spread in a labyrinth, dark and wet, and Gareth handed the torch to Xax, motioning for him to take the lead.

Lane opened her senses, looking for any sign of Eve. She exhaled hard, shaking her head.

"What's the matter?"

She puffed out another breath into the damp. "I can't seem to focus. I need to sense Eve, or we'll end up going in circles."

"That's because you're relying on your witch side. You're a Raven, but you're also a halfling Sidhe, and being where we are, you'll do better tapping into that half."

She snorted. "I don't think this is the place or the time for us to get down and dirty, Gareth."

"I claimed you, love. Your power is right there under the surface for you to try whenever you want. You don't need me anymore." He paused with a gorgeous crooked grin. "Well, not to use your magic anyway. For everything else and for toe-curling, mind-shattering—"

"La, la, la, la...I get the picture," she said singsong, giving him a *shut up now or else* look.

Xax glanced over his shoulder with a long-toothed grin and a snicker on his lips. Lane cocked back, punching Gareth in the shoulder.

"Ow!"

"See?"

He rubbed his arm. "Don't be so uptight. Middle Course is halfway to Faerie, and everyone knows the Fae do it magically."

"Gareth, I swear."

He laughed out loud. "Okay, okay. To save myself some unnecessary bruising, how about you practice your magic. Try an energy ball. Open your hand and concentrate on your palm. Focus. Imagine heat and magic in a blue and white swirl."

She opened her palm as they walked, and a tiny spark formed, but then went out.

"That's a good start. Try again, only this time expand it. Hold the thought."

Lane focused again, and this time the spark held. It swirled in her palm like a tiny blue pulsing galaxy. She blew out a breath, and when she did it spiraled up, growing and coalescing into a sphere.

"Holy shit! Gareth! Look!"

He nodded. "See, I told you. Now wing it at the wall and not my shoulder."

"Ha. Ha." She cocked back, hurling the energy ball against the wall. Rock crumbled in a scorched mess and Xax yelled.

"Are ye crazy? Do ye want to bring the entire substrate down on our heads?"

She flashed what she hoped was a sheepish apology but squealed when Gareth swung his arm around her shoulder.

"Now try a repelling light." He let go of her long enough to palm a handful of rocks from the explosion. "Just concentrate like you did earlier, but instead of thinking destruction, think

prevention. The light should be pure yellow and should buzz in your palm rather than pulse."

She held her hand out again, and this time chanted the word repel over and over in her head. A white light formed, and as it grew it took on a buttery sheen.

It hummed across her skin, and she grinned. "Like holding a glowing vibrator."

"Yeah, well. Don't even think about using it the way I know your dirty mind is thinking. You'll burn your lady bits off."

With a silent wince, she nodded. "Gotcha. Not a toy." Holding her palm up, she barely had time to react when Gareth lobbed a rock at her head.

"Hey!" Instinct kicked in and she ducked. "Send up a smoke signal or something to give me a heads-up there, Golden Boy."

"Nope. What would be the point of that? An opponent isn't going to telegraph his intentions. You have to be ready."

Without warning, he threw another, but this time she recalled her power and changed the rock's trajectory toward the wall instead of her head.

"Very good. Your Sidhe nature is kicking in on a core level. Now try to use that same intuition to sense Eve."

Gareth whistled, grabbing Xax's attention ahead. Xax stopped, and he and Gareth waited while Lane focused her Fae gifts to sense the witch.

She closed her eyes and held both hands out to the side, elbows close. A dull white light emanated over each hand, and it spiraled, circling her skin. The power spread up her arms and across her chest and down until it covered her whole body.

She cocked her head, listening. As though moving on autopilot, she turned on her heel, walking like a glowing Halloween ghost until she stood in front of a stone expanse.

Gareth moved to her side, taking her hand. He hissed as her power surged, clinging to his skin as it merged with his underlying essence.

If ever Xax's fearsome grin could seem approving, it was now. "Warded it be, but tis no wall. Tis a room."

Lane's eyes snapped open. "Eve's inside."

"Our combined blood crumbled the wards at the Red Veil, so maybe we should give that a try."

Gareth fished in his pocket for the mini ritual knife. With a flick, he unfolded the jackknife and held it over her hand.

"I'm really starting to hate this. I'm going to look like a teenage cutter." She winced and held open her palm.

"Stop grumbling. With your Fae abilities, you'll heal even faster now." Gareth sliced her palm and then did the same to himself.

Lane snatched the blade from him. "I'll hang onto this, thank you."

They clasped hands and like before, power sizzled and burned between them. She mumbled the same spell she used at the vampire club and the two let go of each other to smear the wall with their mingled blood.

The stone groaned and cracked, and then dissolved to nothing. No explosion. No earth fissure to swallow the rock expansion. Just poof. Gone.

"Well, that was anticlimactic." No sooner did the words leave Lane's mouth than Leith's undead trio stepped from the shadows.

Hissing, they attacked, the first backhanding Xax, sending him flying into the tunnel wall. The little hogboon goblin hit with a sickening crack, slumping to the ground.

"Eve! She's shackled to the bed! Gareth! Grab her!"

Eve screamed, but Lane kept her eyes on the three vampires as they advanced. Her body shimmered with power, attracting them like moths to a flame.

With a snarl, the first advanced. He moved in a weird shuffle with lips curled over stained fangs.

"Lane! Watch out!"

Gareth raced for the sword on the wall. He yanked it from its bracket, cracking the pommel. "Damn it to hell!"

He fisted the crucifer grip with both hands. Sigils sparked to life despite the crack. He lifted it high with a battle cry, and the blade swung with a spark slicing through Eve's chains.

Freed, she clamored to the corner of the room while he pivoted around to help Lane.

"Over here, leeches!" He sliced the blade over his hand, letting the blood well and drip to the floor in a crimson path. "You want Fae blood, come and get it!"

They turned in unison, their eyes yellow and streaked with black veins.

"It's like an episode of the fucking *Walking Dead*," Lane circled around the other way.

"Yeah, except with fangs."

Gareth gripped the hilt tight, holding his ground until the first vampire closed in with a snarl. He swung the blade, severing its undead head from its shoulders. The others shrieked but kept advancing.

Lane dug in her canvas bag, pulling out a thin metallic net. It glistened in her hand like liquid silver. She swung the precious metal over her head high and wide before throwing fishing net style over the remaining vampires.

They crumpled to the ground, their pallid flesh sloughing in gray ribbons under the silver net.

"Is there anything else in that bag I should know about, Mary Poppins?" Gareth exhaled.

Resting the sword against the wall, he dragged them into the tunnel corridor, leaving them for Rémy. The other had already turned to ash, but at least he'd have these two to use for amends with the Weres.

"Check Xax. I'll get Eve," she said, scanning the room's shadows for her friend.

The room was suddenly alight, and her hand flew to shield her eyes as she squinted, blind.

"Hello, Lane." The voice that spoke her name was definitely male and definitely not Gareth's.

"Who are you?" Her eyes adjusted to see a tall, blond, ethereally beautiful man standing over Eve with his fingers twisted in her dark hair.

He stared at her the same way she stared at him, assessing and wondering. There was no question who he was. They had the same eyes. The same lithe frame.

"Leith." His name was a whispered curse on her tongue.

He inclined his head. "I knew it was only a matter of time before you figured out how to find your friend."

Letting go of Eve's hair, he gave her a rough shove toward the far corner. Her friend cried out, and the sound of her pain tightened Lane's jaw.

Outside, Xax got to his feet despite a small red trickle from the gash at his temple. He shook his

head, holding onto Gareth's arm, but the two turned at Eve's cry.

"Lane!" Gareth let go of the little hogboon goblin, rushing for the room again.

Leith's eyes jerked toward the broken wards, and in seconds white fire shot from both hands, knocking Gareth back toward the tunnel wall.

"Gareth!"

Leith waved one hand, the motion sending Lane crashing toward the pallet bed. Another blitz of pure white fire pinned Gareth to the wall. Then the flash grew, as though feeding on Gareth's own power until there was nothing left. He was gone. No scorch marks. No ashes. Nothing.

"No!"

Pain sluiced through her veins and a shriek ripped from her core. Rage as white hot as Leith's blitz coursed through her veins. She turned for the sword against the wall.

"I wouldn't if I were you, my dear." Leith tsked, holding a short blade to Eve's throat.

Her fingers curled around the hilt. Anger and fear swelled. What should she do? With a snarl, she lifted the sword and plunged it into the dirt. The ground rumbled, opening into a deep crevasse. Dirt and rock crumbled into the gap, but Leith simply laughed. A wave of his hand closed the rift, the ground swallowing the sword with it.

"Little girl, there is so much you need to learn. So much I will teach you once you're at my side."

Her body shook with rage and pain. Heat scorched her palms and she hurled two fireballs at his head. He deflected them with ease, smirking as they barely singed the walls.

All the magic she thought she had at her fingertips was useless against a full Sidhe. Gareth was gone. Her mind rebelled against the thought. This was *not* happening. Yet, here she stood. Facing her father, alone.

Another wave of his hand reset his wards, and just like that, she was cut off from the only way she knew to get home.

Lane steeled her jaw and lifted her eyes to the man who ruined her life. The man responsible for taking everything she loved. The fire Leith used to kill Gareth had hardened her to the core. If he wanted a protégé, he'd get one in spades. At least until she could turn the tables and burn his ass the same way he had the man she loved.

"You took a life. Now it's time to relinquish one," she said, finally.

"You are in no position to bargain, little girl."

"Let Eve go."

He sheathed the knife from her friend's throat and Eve's shoulders slumped.

"Not good enough."

He cocked his head. "Convince me, then."

"Eve served her purpose. She got me here. Now let her go."

He shrugged, and then snapped his fingers. Eve disappeared with a shriek, but it was his laughter that jerked her gaze back to his ice blue eyes.

"Where is she? I said let her go."

"Ah, yes. But you didn't specify *where*."

Lane clenched her fists, ignoring the burning in her palms. She itched to burn his ass, but right now it was futile and a waste of energy. She needed to conserve her resources and feel out the situation.

"Why are you playing games, Leith? You wanted me here, but really, isn't the cost a little high?"

He shrugged. "The cost isn't mine, my dear." He smoothed the front of his velvet coat. "Still, Eve may prove a bargaining chip yet. I sent her to my castle. But don't worry, she has at least three friends there who know her intimately."

If the bastard meant his three bloodsuckers, then obviously, Leith didn't know everything. Not when his vampire mafia was down one head, literally, and the rest were tied up in silver.

Xax would have found Rémy by now, letting him and the others know what happened. Not that they could help.

"Asshole, haven't you heard you catch more flies with honey than vinegar? You want me so badly, you arranged this elaborate scheme, yet

instead of trying to entice me, your first instinct was to frighten and bully me. Dude, it's Machiavellianism 101 in reverse. You always try the sweets before the sour. Then again, my mother said you were good looking. She never said you were smart."

"So, you knew about me."

She shook her head. "Not until yesterday. But I wasn't wrong all these years. You were just a sperm donor."

A slash formed on his lips and his fingers curled. The energy that crackled, though, he extinguished as quickly as it sparked. "You can blame your whore of a mother for that. I was robbed of the chance to be your father, but that is something I plan to remedy."

She nearly laughed in his face. "Well, daddy dearest, you're off to one hell of a start." Lane watched his face, and in that moment, she knew she had him. Not exactly where she wanted, but it was a start.

"You want me for a protégé or whatever? I'll bite, but I have a few conditions."

She'd just learned the hard way about not being specific, and she wasn't about to make the same mistake. She had to out-cunning the master.

"Name your price."

"First, I want Eve safely returned to the motherhouse, unharmed, in one piece, with her

mind and body intact as it was before you took her from the Red Veil.

"Second, I want Gareth restored and returned to the Seelie Court, also unharmed, in one piece, with his mind and body intact before you hit him with your fire ball.

"Next, I want to get a message to Caitlan, the Supreme of the Circle of the Ravens. I want her to know I'm well and staying in Faerie with you of my own volition, and I want the message to be timely. That means Earth time, not Faerie time."

He smirked. "You sound like you've had dealing with the Djinn."

"More like dealings with the cocksucker who sired me. I trust no one and nothing, Leith. From here on in, it's all about me and what I want."

Pride seemed to spark in his eyes, and the smile creeping on his lips made her ill. She dismissed the feeling. There was no time to indulge anything but revenge and getting the hell out of here with the people she loved.

"Oh, and one last thing, Leith."

He inclined his head, waiting.

"I have reason to believe my mother is still alive, and I think you know exactly where she is. I want to see her. Not in a scrying surface or in a memory, but for real, face to face—and she better be healthy and hearty, or hell will reign."

He chuckled, impressed. "How I got you off that wilted rose of a Raven is beyond me. You inherited your mother's pretty face, but there's much more of me in you than you think. You're quick and resourceful, as well as adaptive. Do well to hone those traits." He turned with a flourish. "Very well. If you wish to see your mother, then so be it." He clapped his hands, and in that moment everything went dark.

Chapter Eighteen

*L*ane woke to slatted light winking in from a shuttered window. Blinking to adjust, she tried to sit up, only to wince back against a lumpy pillow.

A dull throb pounded the top of her head in time with nauseous waves in her stomach. She dragged her arm across her eyes, hoping the counterpressure would help.

"Easy now. Give yourself a chance. It'll take a bit for your body to shake off Leith's touch. Gentle isn't a word in his vocabulary."

At the soft feminine voice, Lane pulled her arm back. "If you mean what I think you mean, then he's more of a sick fuck than I thought."

The woman flashed a shy smile. "I haven't heard that accent or that kind of language in a very long time."

Her hand was soft as she brushed Lane's hair back to place a cool towel on her forehead. "He didn't touch you, sweetheart. Not in that way, anyway. He saves that particular cruelty for me."

The woman looked to be in her mid-thirties, with flawless skin and long, sandy blonde hair that

fell to her waist in a thick braid. Her eyes were dove-gray, but dulled, as if all the hope had gone out of her life.

There was something familiar about her, but Lane couldn't place it. Not until the sad woman leaned over to adjust a pillow.

Her pendant came loose from her bodice and swung forward. Lane gripped the woman's arm, all pain and nausea forgotten.

"Is your name Aislinn?" she asked, her eyes taking in every detail of the woman's face.

She nodded but didn't offer anything more.

The door opened and Eve came in carrying a pitcher and washbowl, with a white cloth over her arm.

"Lane!" She rushed forward, water sloshing. "Thank God! Oh, Laney! I knew you'd never give up on me!"

The pitcher and the rest clattered as she dropped them on the nearest table and rushed to give Lane a hug.

Aislinn's eyes went unblinking as the realization hit, and Lane stared at her from over Eve's hug.

"Laney Belle?" She froze with her daughter's hand still on her arm.

Lane's throat tightened against any kind of words, so all she could do was nod.

Eve backed off and stared at the two. "Wait, are you saying this is your…I mean Laney is…"

"Yes, child. To all of the above." Aislinn's voice was barely a whisper as disbelief changed to fleeting joy, but it was regret and censure that took control. She looked away, slipping her arm from Lane's grip.

"No. Don't do that," Lane said, sitting up. "This is not your fault. I chose to be here…and I made him agree to certain conditions. One of them was you."

Aislinn sniffed hard. "You chose to be here. That tells me I failed. Miserably."

Shaken, she got up from the bed and walked toward the window. Pulling back the shutters, she let the room fill with overcast light. "You chose to be here, where it's always either winter or fall."

Aislinn kept her gaze outside. "Caitlan must have given you my letter if you thought to demand anything of your father, let alone to see me."

"That megalomaniac is not my father. He's a sperm donor."

Turning, Aislinn shook her head with a self-disdaining snort. "Then how can I be your mother when I abandoned you?"

"Don't. You did what you did to protect me." Lane got up from the bed, not caring about the cold, damp floor on her bare feet.

"Caitlan did give me your letter. But only because Leith was sniffing around. I know leaving me with the Ravens was the hardest thing you ever had to do. That you stayed with me all that time told me you tried. You weren't wrong about binding my powers."

"But?"

Lane looked at the way the breeze blew loose tendrils around her face. The simple image brought so many memories

"No buts, just a question."

With an inhale, Aislinn lifted her chin, as if bracing herself. "What do you want to know?"

"My only question is why didn't you stay after you and Caitlan bound my Sidhe side? The Circle of the Raven was your home, too. The motherhouse would have protected you as well."

Aislinn looked at the floor. "Seven years on the human plane is barely seven days here in Faerie." She looked up again, her eyes were dry. "Any longer and Leith would have gotten suspicious. I could risk a week, but no more. To be honest, I still can't believe I managed it. Those years with you were the happiest of my life, and the memories have sustained me since."

She moved to crouch by a stone slate near an inside wall. Wiggling the loose rock, she took a metal box from a hole behind the slate.

Aislinn lifted the lid, pulling out a clear plastic bag. "My most precious possessions," she said. "Pictures of you and me."

Lane looked at the mementoes in her mother's hand, and then stared at the woman she remembered, but barely knew. "Stored in an iron strongbox."

"Yes. Hidden but unlocked, because no Fae would dare touch it."

Eve moved to look at the pictures through the Ziplock bag. "Laney, you were so cute. You look just like Aislinn. Even now it's easy to see you're her daughter."

Lane wasn't paying attention. Her eyes hadn't moved from Aislinn's face. "If you knew how to escape home, why didn't you do so beforehand?"

"Leith wasn't always the way he is now. I was happy with him. Happy being here. I barely noticed the changes in him until it was too late. Truth is, I didn't want to leave until he became so cruel and hungry for power there was no way I could let him know about you."

"Then how did he find out about Lane?" Eve asked, handing the pictures back. "Did you tell him?"

Aislinn's eyes went wide. "God, no! He'd have to kill me first."

"Then how?" Eve asked again. "Because his plan to find Lane, and lure her here, was pretty

elaborate for something he'd just learned about. I was taken by mistake. I think he and his cohorts thought Lane would be in that backroom. The club where it all went down is one of her favorite haunts, but he got me instead. Still, everything I suffered is nothing compared to the lives lost in this mess."

Aislinn's eyes welled. "I don't know how he found out about Lane, and I'm so very sorry for everything you two have endured."

Lane unfolded her arms from her chest. "Leith's machinations are not your fault. He's the one responsible. Any normal person who found they had a secret daughter would have contacted me in a normal way. Met me for coffee. Bought me dinner. Not try and kidnap me."

Raking a hand through her hair, she took in the layout of the room. Her gaze moved from the window to the door and then back to both women.

"Eve, you came in with that pitcher and stuff from somewhere outside, so we obviously have the freedom to move around."

"We are at *dun Sliabh Creagach*," Aislinn replied. "It's the seat of Leith's ancestral home. Loosely translated, it means jagged mountain." She swept a hand toward the window.

"Look outside. We're perched on a cliff facing the sea. We have free roam because there's literally nowhere else to go."

Lane moved to the window beside her mother. Aislinn was right about that. The water was dark and beautiful, but despite its majesty, the rocks around the shore were deadly.

She turned abruptly, taking Aislinn's hand. "There has to be another way. Think."

"I don't see how. The portal I used to get home has been sealed since I returned. Leith must have suspected I was testing out an escape, so he had it destroyed. The only other portal is from here to the Seelie Court. We might be able to open it, but they'd never let us through."

"Not even for sanctuary?" Eve asked, nodding as she looked at Lane. "Contrary to what Caitlan thinks, I actually paid attention in class. We could ask for asylum."

Lane dropped her eyes for a moment. "I lost someone dear to me in the Middle Course when we came looking for a way in to rescue Eve. He had sanctuary at the Seelie Court."

Eve moved to Lane's side to take her other hand, and the three of them stood in the stone window overlooking the tumultuous sea.

"I saw what happened during that fight. Who was he, Lane?"

Lane looked up with a sniff. "It was Gareth, Eve. He was the love of my life. Someone I thought lost to this godforsaken plane and this so-called superior race. Leith wasn't the first of his kind to

become drunk on the thought of power." She filled them in on Gareth's story.

"I watched Mason die, too," Eve said, her voice barely a whisper. "It was horrible. And to think I used to think the undead mysterious and sexy. They're nothing but coldhearted predators."

Lane squeezed her hand. "I know, honey. And the undead bastards that helped themselves to his life are getting their hearts and fangs ripped out by their Master Adjudicator. Or at least I hope so. There are a lot of moving parts to this thing.

"We can talk later about the miles of therapy we're facing after we get out of here, but first; we need a plan. We have each other, and we're not without skills. Three Ravens form a circle of three times three times three."

Eve smiled and even giggled the way she used to before this mess. "And you're a halfling Sidhe. So, hell yeah. I'm in."

"How?" Aislinn voiced. "I just said there's no portal open to us, even to the Middle Course. Only the Seelie Court."

Lane nodded. "Exactly. And I'm wearing Gareth's claim." She lifted her palm, showing them the sigil. "When he was alive it shimmered translucent gold, but since the Middle Course…"

Her voice trailed, and she let go of Eve's hand to run a finger over the dull white scar. "Well, at least it's still a pretty design."

"It's beautiful, Lane." Eve took her hand again.

"Yes." She nodded again. "Let's hope it's also our ticket out of here. Maybe it'll give Leith a stroke that someone laid claim to me first." She smiled.

Aislinn loosed her hand from their strategizing. "If we're really going to do this, then we don't have much time. In this castle, servants' eyes and ears are everywhere. Eve and I managed to ward this room to give us some privacy, but only just barely. The manor is like a trip wire. Anything but a gossamer touch sets off alarms."

"God, that man is not just a megalomaniac, he's paranoid as shit." Lane exhaled a disgusted grunt.

"He is what he is, Laney Belle. We can't worry about that now. He has plans for you. I know him, sweetheart. He won't want to wait. The servants have most likely let him know you've stirred from the portal's magical backlash. Everyone thinks it's so easy for the Fae to abduct unwilling victims. It's not. It takes as much out of them as it does the abductee."

"You sound almost sorry he suffered dragging me and Eve here." Lane paused, sparing a look for Eve.

"Aislinn, if you have any doubts, you have to voice them now. We can't have you go all Stockholm Syndrome on us at the last minute."

Her mother shook her head. "I'm in. If only to get you two back where you belong. I don't really care about me."

"You should. Just because your lover changed course mid-trip doesn't mean you're obligated to ride the crazy train with him." Eve nodded. "Besides, you look amazing. You left the human realm twenty years ago, but you don't look like you've aged at all."

Aislinn patted Eve's arm. "I've aged all right. Mentally and emotionally. Even if the packaging is well preserved."

"Good genes." Lane slipped her arm around Aislinn's shoulders. "Like mother, like daughter."

Lane pecked her mother's cheek and then left their huddle to hunt for her clothes.

"They're not here, honey," Aislinn said. "Leith wants us all to dress in Fae fashion."

She sat on the end of the bed, scrubbing the heel of her palm into her eye. "Great. So, we all look like extras from the Lord of the Rings."

"I thought Renaissance Festival, but either works," Eve said, opening the wardrobe. "C'mon, Laney. At least they're pretty. Think of it like playing dress-up."

Lane exhaled, but then squared her shoulders and got up from the bed. "Maid Marion does manslaughter," she mumbled.

Dressed and ready to play their parts, the three women sat in the manor's courtyard. Leith hadn't showed yet and waiting ratcheted the tension for everyone.

"Maybe he knows and isn't coming," Eve whispered, holding her needlepoint. "And what the hell is it you've got me sewing? I'm a twenty-first century witch, not a homespun hack."

"Shut it, Eve. Until we have lift off, just play the game. He thinks this is a cat and mouse, but he's about to find out he's up against a pride of lionesses and he's lunch." Lane gripped the wooden frame of her needlepoint so tightly it cracked.

The overcast sky had broken into a dull sunshine. A cool breeze off the water stirred the sheer trim on Lane's dress, and she frowned. Under any other circumstances, she'd love this level of cosplay. But this gave new meaning to the term ladies-in-waiting.

Footsteps echoed from the main house, and Aislinn looked up from her sewing, giving a nearly imperceptible nod.

"Lane, I'm heartened to see you dressed as a lady of your station. You are of house, *dun Sliabh Creagach*, and all will know you as such." He frowned, turning his attention to Aislinn as she helped Eve pull a stray thread.

"Don't grow too contented with your daily comforts, you unworthy whore. You are only here

because my daughter wishes it. That's right, you taint-blooded slut. *My* daughter. The one you hid from me and then abandoned."

He walked behind her, giving her hair a vicious yank, pulling her from her chair. Aislinn winced, but she didn't cry out.

A servant took a step toward her as she lay on the ground beside her chair, but one look from Leith sent the girl running. He waved his hand and every servant fled.

Lane flung her broken sewing at Leith and rushed to Aislinn's side, motioning for Eve to follow. The two crouched beside her, helping her to her feet.

"I guess you didn't take my hint about flies and honey, did you, asshole? What an absolute waste. Like Mama said, you might look like a sexy, real-life Legolas, but you're no Lord of the Rings. You're nothing. Not to me and not to her."

"Really, dearest. I expected more of you."

Lane straightened, keeping her hand linked with Aislinn's. Eve stood on the opposite side, her fingers laced as well.

"Are you addressing me or my mother? She was your dearest once, but that all changed when you decided to try for glory. I've got news for you, bucko. For glory you need guts, and you are nothing but an insecure little boy trying to fill a man's shoes."

"Rail all you want, Lane. In time, the lure of your Sidhe blood will be too strong to resist." With a snort, he turned on his heel. "I'll leave you to your happy reunion, but come morning we have a war to plan, and I expect my daughter to be at my side and do and say everything I ask, or this reunion will be a funeral pyre."

"Time's up, dude. My Sidhe blood is calling and it wants you!"

The three Ravens lifted their joined hands, with Lane at their center. Power grew, circling and swirling in and through the circle of three.

Leith growled, lifting his hands, but his palms were empty. His eyes flashed to Lane and she pushed her lips to a vengeful smirk. "Your biggest flaw is hubris, Leith. Not mendacity. Not avarice. But pride and overconfidence. You left the three of us to our own devices, gave us freedom to walk the halls of this manor. What you forgot is we're witches, and when you get three of us together, we can open a whole can of whoop ass."

Aislinn smiled. "All those years you kept me sequestered didn't dull my witchy powers. I practiced alone. Honing my skills. Hoping one day you'd grow so complacent, so sure of my yolk you'd forget the rule of three and unwittingly bring other witches here. I should thank you, Leith. Not only did you bring me witches, but you brought

Ravens, and no one masters the power of three times three times three better."

Lane nodded. "There's one other tidbit you should know. The rules also ricochet. Whatever you put into the universe will come back threefold."

Eve giggled her sweet laugh. "Basically, dude, you're fucked."

Aislinn turned, blowing in the direction of the crystals they placed in a circle ahead of time. The exact circle where Leith stood.

The pure quartz blazed with white light, and he turned in a rush, but he was trapped.

"Tsk, tsk, Dad. Game's over and you lose."

"I am an immortal! You cannot kill me!"

They gripped hands even tighter. Their words catching power, it eddied within the bound circle.

"We call the realms of space and time, unlock the gates, release the prime. From fiery breath, world's first light, fire burn and candle bright, invoke the fates, set wrongs to right, burn baby burn, our foe now smite!"

The courtyard's bluestone slates shook and split. Leith fell to his knees as around him the ground gave way. It crumbled like it did in the Middle Course, only this time Leith couldn't seal the rift. Fire spewed all around him as he knelt on a small outcrop of rock.

Lane pulled loose from Eve's grip, keeping her other hand laced with her mother's hand. They'd do this together.

She lifted a hand toward the fiery rock, and mumbled words she didn't know she knew. Wind ripped and swirled and in the midst of the maelstrom, the sword rose.

Calling to it, she gripped the hilt and with every ounce of strength, hurled the iron clad steel into Leith's chest.

He screamed as the iron ore flamed, engulfing his body in the one fire no full Sidhe could withstand. He fell to the depths, white flame sealing his fate. Lane waved a hand over the pit, and it sealed.

"Huh. I guess like father like daughter."

Aislinn squeezed her hand, before pressing a kiss to her daughter's cheek. "Let's not build on that, okay?"

Lane laughed. "Like mother like daughter."

"Uhm, can we make like a banana and split? I don't want to be here when the minions find out we toasted their boss."

Aislinn nodded. "C'mon. The portal to the Seelie Court is down by the water."

"The water! You mean down those rocks?" Eve stopped short.

Bewitch Me

"Did you think Leith would make any part of this easy?" She tugged Eve's sleeve. "We'll be fine. I know a shortcut."

Chapter Nineteen

"Gareth claimed you." It wasn't a question. Still, it didn't bode well to ignore the Seelie queen. Not in her own court, anyway.

"Yes, your Grace. He did." Lane lifted her hand to show the queen the mark on her palm.

The queen beckoned her closer, and when in reach she touched the dull white mark softly. "That's quite a sigil. Gareth must have loved you very much."

Lane nodded, swallowing against the lump in her throat. "As I him."

The queen considered Lane, waving her back to her place. "A claiming rite is a varied and personal thing. It can be simple and perfunctory or elaborate and heartfelt. It requires only two things, of which I'm sure you're aware."

Lane bobbed her head, not trusting her voice.

"Do you recall any of the words spoken when Gareth claimed you?" She gestured toward the sigil. "The words he used ensuring the rite."

Gareth's words were a tattoo on her heart, even as the sentiments behind them were evidenced on her hand. "Every word, your Grace."

"Can you repeat them for me?"

Lane stifled a recoil. The woman wasn't just the Tiana, Queen of the Seelie, Sovereign of the Summer Court. She was *all* Sidhe. As selfish and thoughtlessly forbidding as Leith was cruel.

"I'd rather not, your Grace. Gareth's words are still too painful to remember, let alone speak aloud."

The queen looked at her, but then lifted a dismissive hand. "Indulge me."

Jaw set, Lane glanced away for a moment. Every eye in the court was on her now, and she dare not refuse. Not if she wanted the woman on the throne to allow her, Eve, and Aislinn to return home in one piece.

She sucked in a breath, ignoring the anger and hurt stinging her eyes. *"Root of my root, star spun lives. Bound in flesh and spirit light. Blood of my blood, bone of my bone, I claim thee now as we are one. United in life, transcended in death, the claim is cast on Danu's breath."*

"Thank you, Lane. Your lover's words were as I suspected. He was and is a very clever halfling. It's why I welcomed him to my court. Aside from the fact he's rather yummy to look at."

Flummoxed, Lane blinked at the regal woman. "Was and *is*, your Majesty? Gareth is dead."

She smiled, showing perfect white teeth behind full lips. "Ah, there's dead and then there's dead-dead."

Lane's pulsed raced in that moment. Tiana had uttered the exact words Gareth said when she first saw him at the Red Veil.

"I see by your eyes you understood my meaning, or at least partly. When Gareth spoke the words, *united in life, transcended in death*, he unwittingly found a loophole. He spent enough time in Faerie to know we are cunning creatures, and unless requests are made comprehensively, it leaves room for less exacting interpretations. Wiggle room, to use a human phrase, that the Sidhe employ at their whim."

Lane licked her lips, afraid to ask the million-dollar question biting her tongue. Leith had played the same game when she demanded he let Eve go. She assumed he understood she meant home to the motherhouse. The bastard was true to his nature and played her.

When the queen didn't elaborate, Lane plucked up the courage and asked, "Are you telling me Gareth is alive?"

Tiana lifted a hand again. "Not exactly. Not yet."

She motioned for Lane to approach again, and when she was close enough, the queen took Lane's hand, holding it palm up. She beckoned one of her ladies-in-waiting forward and took a silver and jewel encrusted dirk from the woman's belt.

Without preamble, the queen slit Lane's palm below the claiming sigil. Blood rose in a red line, and Lane didn't dare move. Tiana then did the unthinkable. She pricked her own finger and held it over Lane's palm.

The collective gasp that rose from the court earned a stern eyebrow from the queen, and it quieted immediately.

She curled her finger inward, waiting. "You'll have to forgive the court, my dear. They are not used to witnessing my aid to halflings and Ravens, but if we are to survive the new millennium and continue to thrive, that needs to change.

"My counterpart, Lachlan, King of the Unseelie and Sovereign of the Winter Court, wholeheartedly agrees. It's the reason Leith attempted his coup. He knew that with you and your mother, he had an ace up his sleeve. Who better to rule a new dynastic Faerie than one who had…what is it you humans say? Skin in the game?"

The queen then uncurled her finger. "Do you know where Gareth fell?" she asked.

Lane nodded. "In the labyrinths of the Middle Course near the abandoned spring portal."

"Very well. Picture him there. Not as he was when Leith set him aflame, but as you wish to see him. Virile. Handsome. Whole. Keep the image vivid, and do not pull away from my hand." Her eyes met Lane's and her gaze held.

Lane nodded and then closed her eyes as instructed. Without hesitation, Tiana squeezed the tip of her finger. A drop of royal blood mingled with the blood in Lane's palm.

Immediate pain shot through Lane's hand, scorching worse than any burn from a hot stove.

A strangled cry died on her tongue as she gritted her teeth against the reflex to jerk away. Lane didn't dare open her eyes, betting her flesh had crisped, charring as the agony spread toward her elbow.

Panting, she concentrated on Gareth, forcing her mind to a place of cool water and refreshing breezes. She pictured Gareth's sexy crooked grin, and the way his raspberry blue eyes flashed with laughter. The way those same blue eyes darkened with need as his body tensed with desire. The image expanded, and memories of him flooded her mind and heart, augmenting the picture in her head, making the pain subside.

In that moment, the queen released her hand. Lane opened her eyes, expecting worse than third degree burns, only to find her skin smooth and unmarked.

"I'm sorry, my dear, but I had to test you. I actually got the idea from a Sci-Fi book decades ago." She waved her hand dismissively. "I can't recall the title, and it doesn't really matter, though I admit, the method is quite effective."

Lane's mouth dropped. "You gave me a Fae version of the *Bene Gesserit* box test from *Dune*?

"Gareth proved his love for you by sacrificing his life for yours. If I am to help bring him back from the dead, I need to be sure you are deserving of my help. Though you professed as much, I needed to satisfy you truly love him as you sat." She smiled. "You passed the test."

Lane rubbed the phantom burning still in her hand. "Well, thanks. I guess."

The queen inclined her head again.

"So, your Grace. What now?" Lane threw caution and propriety to the wind. If Tiana was psycho enough to magically duplicate a fictional torture device, then nothing was certain. "How do you help bring Gareth back? He's a Phoenix, so his DNA might prove helpful. The last time it took ten years."

The queen shook her head. "Much less than that. A month in Faerie, and he was sitting up in bed. Of course, it took many months for him to fully regain his strength. His DNA, as you put it, allowed him to return from the ashes because he was killed

with human flame. This time he was killed with Fae fire. It's a little trickier."

"How long for him to recover this time, your Grace? Just give it to me straight."

The queen raised an eyebrow, but the smirk tugging at the corner of her mouth said she was impressed.

"Very well. The images you held in your mind during your trial are all that was required." She motioned to Lane's palm. "Your sigil. See how it glows iridescent, instead of the flat white as when you arrived at my court? Your trial had you endure simulated Fae fire, but it was your strength of will and your love for Gareth that sustained you. Not only did you prove your faithfulness to me, you proved it to the fates. Gareth lives. He will need to recover but seek him where last you saw him. He will be there."

Lane's heart pounded with every word the queen spoke, and every fiber of her being twisted to bolt for the nearest portal, but she didn't dare turn and run.

As if reading her mind, Tiana lifted a hand. "What are you waiting for, girl? Go!"

Lane pivoted on her heel, but then stopped, circling back to offer a curtsey. She caught Eve and Aislinn's faces in the flurry. How could she go anywhere knowing they were still stuck?

Holding her breath, Lane straightened. "Your Grace," she began haltingly. "What about my friend and my mother?"

"It is my wish they stay at court a little longer. Rest assured they will be restored to you in due time." The queen turned her eyes to Aislinn. "I believe there is much to learn from your mother about resolve."

Lane hesitated, but then plunged ahead. "Would due time be in Fae time or *our* time?"

The queen laughed out loud, her eyes flashing gold. "Do you really want to ask that question of me?"

"No, ma'am. I guess not." Lane shook her head. "I'll have to trust you and your word."

Tiana gestured to one of her guards. "Ilar, escort Mistress Alden to the spring portal. You will follow her to the Middle Course, but no farther. Report back to me once you return."

The guard's fist hit his breastplate. "As you wish, your Grace."

Lane curtsied low, mouthing the words thank you before turning for the door with the guard. She followed him down the palace steps and into the palace park.

The gardens were wild and beautiful, with every kind of tree and flowering plant known and unknown in an endless summer. No wonder the

Sidhe picked the New York Botanical Gardens to hide portals and ex-pat fae.

Ilar led her to a spring at the center of a temple-like garden. Water lilies floated on thick green stalks in the dark depths. Trees reflected on the surface gave all who looked a magical mirror image.

"This spot is beautiful and all, but what do we do next?" Lane waited for Ilar as he stood by the silty edge, silent.

"Are you telling me you don't know how to work this inter-realm thingamajig, because I certainly don't. Gareth and I had a hogboon helping us—" she broke off mid-sentence as Xax's words to Gareth came flooding back.

She met the guard's eyes. "What's your name again?"

"Ilar, mistress."

"Well, Ilar. Do you guys know the *Ballad of Tam Lin*?"

"Of course, mistress," he replied. "It's a well-loved tale."

She nodded, chewing on her lip. "Okay, then I think I know how to start our engines here. I need the words to the last lines of that poem, and a silver blade."

He stood blinking, as if unsure what to do next. "Chop, chop!" She clapped her hands. "Pen and paper, or quill and parchment. Whatever floats

your Faerie boat. I don't know this ballad, so I'll need you to dictate the exact words so I can write them down."

Ilar turned on his heel and jogged in the direction of the palace. When he came back, he had a rolled piece of parchment and what looked like Gareth's ritual jackknife in his hand.

"Will these suffice, mistress?"

Lane took the knife from his hand. It was Gareth's all right. "Where did you get this?"

Her voice cracked at the thought of Gareth's belongings traded for bets on dice games in some dank garrison.

"The queen gave it to me earlier. She said if you asked for a blade, I was to give you this. The parchment I had to procure."

He held out the scroll. "It is the ballad in its entirety. My mother wrote out the poem for me when I was a lad."

Guilt bit at her for thinking the worst. "I'm sorry for snapping at you, Ilar. I appreciate the help. I promise I'm not keeping the poem. I just need to recite the words."

He nodded and unrolled the parchment, holding it up for her to see. "Whenever you're ready, mistress."

Lane issued a silent prayer to the universe and ran her thumb over the delicate runes and Celtic scrolling on the jackknife's handle.

"Here goes everything." Opening Gareth's blade, she traced a five-point star in the air as she read the last lines of the *Ballad of Tam Lin*.

"Oh, had I known, Tam Lin," she said, *"what this knight I did see, I have looked him in the eyes and turned him to a tree."*

The water in the spring rippled then swirled until it settled again, showing clear as glass. At the bottom was the torchlit passage where Gareth shielded her from Leith's energy ball.

Her chest tightened at the memory, and dry tears scored her throat. She blinked back the sting, peering into the crystal water for any sign of Gareth.

Blue and white flame had consumed his body in seconds. The ball of energy left nothing behind. No scorch marks, and no ash.

"He's not there," she murmured to herself.

Ilar stepped to her side, rolling the scroll before sticking it into his breastplate. "Are you sure this is the place you last saw him?"

She nodded. "We had come down that passage, there, with Xax." Gesturing toward the stone tunnel, she shrugged. "The hogboon helped us."

"Then perhaps the exiled goblin found your mate and is tending him now."

Lane went up on tip toe and pecked the man's scruffy cheek. "You, Ilar, are a genius." She gripped the guard's hand and stepped to the edge of the

spring. "Let's go. I have a hogboon goblin to find. On the count of three, jump."

Chapter Twenty

*L*ane held tight to Ilar's arm. The membrane between realms was translucent and thin as they crossed the boundary from Faerie into the Middle Course. The feel was gossamer as they passed, the same filmy consistency as when she crossed with Gareth from the human plane through the rock portal near the lilac grove.

Ilar landed without noise or disturbing the soft ground, holding tight to Lane to keep her from pitching forward into the stone.

She caught her breath and found her feet before letting go of his arm. She looked around at the ground, and the telltale signs of the fight that ensued a week ago. Or was it a day? Leith had killed Gareth in this spot, but Lane had no clue if time in the Middle Course ran concurrent with Faerie or with the human realm.

"Is it always so cold here?" Ilar asked, brushing residual film from his arms.

Lane didn't reply. There was no sign of Gareth or Xax, and that meant she needed to look for them.

Or at the very least, find her way to the rock portal and hope she found her happy ending.

"Look," she said, turning toward the Fae guard. "The spring portal won't reseal itself with the spell I used. I can close it now, but then you'd be stuck here. I know you have to get back to Faerie and report to the queen."

"Couldn't you use the same spell to reopen the portal once you've found your mate?"

She shrugged. "I don't know. To be honest, the fact it worked at all was a shot in the dark. Fact is, we both can't leave the portal unattended. I need you to stay here. Guard the opening against gatecrashers. I'll go ahead and find my hogboon friend. I'm sure he can help with portal magic."

Ilar shook his head. "The queen ordered I accompany you."

"I know, but the portal is wide open. Anyone could enter and I don't want to take the chance. The queen's new philosophies regarding halflings and Ravens didn't strike me as popular among her courtiers. Stay here. Guard the portal. I promise, I'll be back."

She hesitated, turning back with Gareth's knife. "Take this. It belonged to my mate, and it means the world to me. Keep it until I get back."

He looked at the small knife and then nodded, his face telling her he understood it was collateral.

She pecked Ilar's cheek again and then took off through the tunnel, hunting for anything Xax left behind for her to follow.

The hogboon had dropped cherry blossom petals Hansel and Gretel style the first time they passed this way. Lane flicked her palm open, and a ball of light swirled, illuminating the passage.

Xax's petals were still there, brown and mushy, but still fragrant enough in the rock enclosure.

Giving Ilar Gareth's blade meant she didn't have it to trace a pentacle in the air if she needed it to open the crevice in the rock portal. Xax would never leave it open, not with Eesa still weak.

The walls of the stone labyrinth seemed claustrophobic, and she needed to stop and recheck the ground or risk losing her way in the maze. The petals Xax left were crushed into the dirt, making them hard to see.

"C'mon, Lane. You're a halfling Sidhe and a Raven witch. Double the power. The Fae are connected to nature, do something. Think."

She closed her eyes and mumbled an improvised rhyme. It was juvenile, but perhaps it would do the trick. *Light of day in the midst of night, Petals soft white and bright.*

Cringing at the half-assed spell, she waited with the ball of light pulsing in her hand. Sparks broke off in a swirl, floating to the dirt floor. One by one old petals plumped, their tender white satin

glowing in a definite line leading to the outer portal.

"Damn! It's good to be a witchy Sidhe!"

Not wasting another second, Lane took off running. Her footfalls echoed off the stone, and her breath puffed in short cloudy pants. She rounded a corner only to skid to a stop when she saw Xax waiting at the open crevice.

"I'm not sure what ye did, mistress, but the whole of the grove is alight with magic. Blooms across cherry trees and the lilacs both are aglow, so I knew ye'd returned."

He made a tight flourished bow, and she couldn't resist rubbing his dobby-like ears. "You, my friend, are a sight for sore eyes. Please, tell me...is he...is..." her throat tightened, and she couldn't bring herself to ask.

Xax took her hand, careful to keep his taloned fingers loose. "He's here, mistress. Weak. But whole again and aching for ye." He pulled her toward the opening. "Come."

"I—" She hesitated, glancing over her shoulder. "The queen sent someone to help me. He's watching the spring portal. I know you have reasons not to cross paths with the queen's guard, and after all you've done for me, I won't bring trouble to your doorstep."

Xax's ear's flicked toward the direction she came, and his nose twitched. "I have nothing to

fear, mistress. Not on this side of the portal. My exile is not the queen's concern. It was the Unseelie's doing."

He lifted her hand, giving it another tug. "Leave the guard be and come see your love."

Heart pounding, she let the Hogboon lead. When they exited the crevice, the entire lesser Fae population was there to greet them. Gareth stood at the center of the throng. Tall and gorgeous as ever and wearing a sexy crooked smile.

"Gareth!"

Jerking free of Xax's hand, Lane ran toward him, not caring the lesser Fae had to jump or risk being flattened.

"You're alive! Thank God!" She flung herself into his arms, the force sending his breath from his chest in a soft whoomph.

He laughed, wincing from the vise grip hug. "Easy, love. I'm not quiet one hundred percent."

Crying, Lane buried her face in his chest. "Don't you ever do that to me again!"

His chest vibrated with a soft chuckle. "What? Die or save your life?"

"Just shut up, Golden Boy, and kiss me!"

His mouth crushed hers and he lifted her off her feet, spinning her around. Lane poured everything into their kiss. Fear, anger, worry, sadness, joy, and most of all, love.

Putting her down, he stepped back when her feet touched the ground. His eyes took in every inch of her tearstained face. "I knew you'd figure it out," he said, wiping her cheeks.

"I didn't, actually. It was Tiana. She's the one who knew you'd be smart enough to find a loophole to cheat death by Fae fire."

He smiled. "She's really something."

"I guess. Even if she's decided to keep Eve and my mother in Faerie a bit longer. She says they can teach her a lot about human resolve."

"Resolve?"

Lane nodded. "She's adopting a new policy on inter-Fae relations."

"Uh oh," he winced, but not from pain.

"Uh oh is right. To be honest, she's a little scary. Fickle and unpredictable."

Gareth cocked his head, surprised. "What did you expect, Lane? A straight shooter? Tiana is the Queen of the Sidhe, and that makes her queen manipulator."

"I know, but I didn't expect her to be so stereotypically Sidhe one moment and magnanimous the next. I still can't believe she helped bring you back. She even sent a personal guard to ensure I got here from Faerie in one piece. He's still at the spring portal watching for gatecrashers. I had to give him your jackknife as collateral or he wouldn't stay put. The last thing I

wanted was for him to scare Xax or the other exiles."

Gareth glanced past her shoulder to the open crevice at the rock portal. "Then we'll have to go back together and show your friend it's mission accomplished. You need to close the portal anyway after he leaves, and if I know Tiana, she's already waiting for her detailed report."

"Well, you certainly know Tiana. And she knows you."

He looked at her funny. "What's that supposed to mean?"

Lane chewed her lip as the lesser Fae dispersed back to the grove. Gareth nodded to Xax as he and Eesa stood by their tree. Lane blew them a kiss, touching a hand to her heart as Gareth took her hand to walk down the slope to the narrow crevice in the rock face.

"Gareth, you were one of the queen's favorites, right?"

He shrugged. "Tiana has many pets, but I suppose she liked me well enough. She helped me return from the dead so you and I could be together, so yeah."

"Did you and she, you know—" Lane let the question just lay there.

"So that's where your last comment came from. Did Tiana and I, what? What is it you're stumbling over your tongue to ask?"

Lane felt her cheeks flush, but seeing Tiana, she had to know. "After everything we've been through, you're really going to make me spell it out?"

He didn't reply, and she growled low in frustration.

"Fine. I'm a big girl, so I'm just going to ask. I want to know if the Seelie queen took advantage of her position and made you do her—"

"What? Bidding?"

Lane let go of his hand. "No, you big jerk! *Her*! Did you do HER?"

"Oh, man. You're jealous! I die and get brought back from the ether and all you're worried about is if I slept with the Faerie queen?"

"I am not jealous." She sniffed. "Tiana is a beautiful sovereign who's used to getting everything she wants the moment she wants it. No one tells her no." She looked at him. "So, did you?"

"You didn't wonder about my connection with the queen when you knew she sent me to help with Leith, so why now?"

Lane folded her arms tight. "Because she gave me the Fae version of the *Bene Gesserit* box test!"

"Like from *Dune?*" His mouth dropped.

"It's not funny, Gareth! I thought the woman deep fried my hand!"

Gareth tugged her close again, but she kept her arms crossed even in his embrace.

"I'm sorry, Laney. Tiana can be capricious and even cruel sometimes, but she's better than most."

"She handed me some bull about being sure I was worthy of you. That my love for you was just as fierce as yours was for me." She sniffed again, before lifting her face to his. "Was it torture for sport, or compensation for letting you go? Or just for shits and giggles to see how much I would withstand to have you?"

He kissed the top of her head, resting his cheek on her hair. "I don't know, love. It could be all of the above, or nothing at all. Fae who only know their own realm are a funny lot. Maybe Tiana keeping Eve and Aislinn is a good thing. Either way, your suffering got the job done. Even from nothingness, I felt every emotion. As strong as they are right now with you in my arms. I knew whatever you poured into that magic, it would work."

Lane exhaled an acquiescent breath. "I suppose I should be grateful you were favorite enough for her to want you to be happy. Now if we could only parlay that into her letting my mother and Eve come home. They're Ravens, not lab rats."

He lifted her chin so he could see her eyes. "We can."

"How? I love you, Gareth, but I'm not doing the fry daddy thing again."

He laughed for a moment, but then his face softened. "We go back to the Summer Court, together. We ask the queen for an indulgence. Tiana might insist we stay in exchange for Eve and Aislinn, but then they have the choice to either stay with us or return. Either way, you and I will be together. And if we stay in Faerie, that together is a very, very long time."

She grinned up at him, loosening her arms to fit around his waist. "Long. As in forever, right?"

"My bewitching love, anything is possible with you."

Epilogue

"*L*ane, seriously hope this isn't some macabre, visit-the-scene-of-the-crime, fetish thing."

"Trust me, Gareth. You're the one who said that thinking about the time I spent in the backrooms was a turn on."

"Yeah, that was before I saw what they did to that poor Were kid."

Lane nodded. "I know. From what Rémy said, Sean Leighton was not happy at all. He nearly ripped up the truce because Rémy kept it from him so long."

"I don't blame him, but there were extenuating circumstances, plus the Vampire Council gave Sean his due. He watched as they sent those two demented vampers to final death, without their fangs."

"I don't want to talk about it anymore. It's over. Eve and my mother are visiting Caitlan, while you and I are here. So, let's enjoy ourselves before we head back."

"Remember we promised Xax and Eesa we'd stop at the bakery for them."

"I know. Chocolate croissants in gold foil paper. I don't know which Xax wants more. The pastry or the wrapper."

She stopped in front of a silver door with a spray of rhinestones. "Yay! We're here."

"Where? Elvis's dressing room?"

Up on tip toe, she pressed a kiss to his lips, letting it linger. "No, babe. It's my favorite fantasy room of all. Glitter Kink. Sexy burlesque with a twist."

She stepped back from him and let her long, thin leather coat puddle to her ankles.

"Holy fuck-me pumps! Lane, what the—? You wore that under your coat on the subway!" He licked his lips at the strappy, crotchless leather and rhinestone bikini and stiletto heels.

Before he could say another word, she took the feather boa from her neck and wrapped it around his waist, tugging him toward the door.

"Leather and sexy, glittery toys enough to make any woman spread wide and wet and sigh…" She smiled, crooking her little finger. "Come play, Gareth. I promise, it'll be something you never forget."

"Bewitch me, baby. All the way."

Marianne Marea

Like FREEBIES and SWAG and info on contests and new releases? SIGN UP FOR MY MONTHLY NEWSLETTER!
http://www.mariannemorea.com/contact-me.html

If you enjoyed the story, please feel free to email me. Reviews are always welcome, especially on Amazon, iBooks and Goodreads!

About the Author

 Marianne Morea was born and raised in New York. Inspired by the dichotomies that define 'the city that never sleeps', she began her career after college as a budding journalist. Later, earning a MFA, from The School of Visual Arts in Manhattan, she moved on to the graphic arts. But it was her lifelong love affair with words, and the fantasies and 'what ifs' they stir, that finally brought her back to writing.

More by Marianne Morea

THE RED VEIL DIARIES

(Reading Order)

Choose Me
Tempt Me
Tease Me
Taste Me
Bewitch Me
*Charm Me

THE CURSED BY BLOOD SAGA

Hunter's Blood (Shifter Romantic Suspense!)

Fever Play (Short, fast, and HOT!)

Twice Cursed (Vamp/Were…Book hangover possible!)

Blood Legacy (Icy hot vamp romance)

Lion's Den (Will make you cry happy tears!)

Power Play (Hot and Suspenseful!)

Collateral Blood (Vampire Suspense!)

Condemned (Vampire Suspense!)

Of Blood and Magic (Vampire/Witch Suspense!)

THE LEGEND SERIES (Teen)

Hollow's End (Witch Suspense)

Time Turner (Time Travel Suspense)

Spook Rock (Ghost Suspense)

THE BLESSED

My Soul to Keep (Angels and Demons)

MT PRESS BOOKS

Sass Master
(Sassy Ever After-The Catamount Shifters)

Lucky Sass
(Sassy Ever After-The Catamount Shifters)

Sass in the City
(Sassy Ever After-The Catamount Shifters)

HOWLS ROMANCE

Her Fairytale Wolf
(Modern twist on Cinderella)

The Wolf's Dream Mate
(Modern twist on Sleeping Beauty)

Her Winter Wolves
(Modern twist on Snow White)

The Alpha's Chase
(Marriage of Convenience)